DARCY

Boyfriend For Hire, Book 1

RJ SCOTT
MEREDITH RUSSELL

Love Lane Books

Darcy, Boyfriend for Hire, 1

Copyright © 2018 RJ Scott, Copyright © 2018 Meredith Russell

Cover design by Meredith Russell, Edited by Sue Laybourn

Published by Love Lane Books Limited

ISBN - 9781785645396

All Rights Reserved

Dedication

For our family and friends.

Boyfriend for Hire
DARCY

RJ SCOTT & MEREDITH RUSSELL

Love Lane Books

Chapter One

Spring in New York was magical.

The snow had gone, and the bitter edge of a vicious March had subsided enough that Darcy Bridges could spend time in the park and not have to worry about freezing his ass on the bench. April was a quiet time in Stuyvesant Street, with blossoms on the trees, and the winter ground of the tiny park in the middle had been transformed by an explosion of green.

Also, it wasn't too hot yet. Not in that New York way where the tourists complained and the natives were irritable. In the heat, the horns were louder, and irritation was quick to turn to anger, until every journey across the city was a nightmare of epic proportions.

Sitting on the bench, throwing the crumbs of a BLT from the deli to the waiting birds, was Darcy's idea of heaven. Peace, nature, and the silence of being away from his Brooklyn apartment was exactly what he needed today.

Too much had happened to him over the last ten years for him to ever appreciate the vibrant noise of the city. He rubbed his knee thoughtfully as he watched the pigeons squabble over what he'd thrown and waited for Rowan Phillips to come for him.

"Thought I'd find you here," Rowan said from behind and then climbed over the seat to sit on the back.

What is it about my friend that makes him unable sit on a bench like a normal person?

"I always wait here," Darcy explained for the fiftieth time of this happening.

"Yeah, I know." Rowan bumped a knee to Darcy's shoulder. "But I had to say something to warn you I was coming so I didn't scare the shit out of you and had you rolling to cover a nonexistent grenade like some kind of superhero."

Darcy side-eyed him. "You're an asshole. Once. I did that *once*."

"Whatever, dude. I'm just being a good best friend." Rowan grinned at him and kneed him again.

"Stop with the kneeing, you child," Darcy groused and then pushed back at Rowan, who would have fallen off the end of the bench if it hadn't been for the wrought iron armrest he caught as he began to tumble. He huffed and brushed off imaginary dirt. They'd been like this since they were kids, growing up in a blink-and-it's-gone small town in Maine, next door neighbors, and kind-of-boyfriends for one shining hour in the summer of ninety-nine.

Rowan was the one who'd had Darcy's back in kindergarten when bullies had decided Darcy was a target and warranted him being picked on. But when Darcy grew taller and stronger, it was *his* turn to have Rowan's back when Rowan came out at the age of fifteen. Darcy had taken longer to announce his sexuality to his confused mom. Confused because she'd said she'd always known, and what the hell was he telling her for? Oh, and did he have a boyfriend yet?

He enlisted into the army at seventeen, while Rowan went to college then took up a career in pharmaceutical sales, post-graduation.

When Rowan had suffered from a burnout, Darcy had been in Iraq. When Darcy's parachute had twisted and he'd fucked up his knee, Rowan had been on a retreat in India working on his chakras. But they always found their way back to each other as best friends.

They'd made it here though, together. Rowan, a PA for a man who was happy to put up with his frequent flights of fancy, and Darcy a pivotal member of the same company.

Bryant & Waites. Boyfriends for hire. Not an escort agency, although what happened on a job, stayed on a job, obviously. Run by the enigmatic Gideon from an expensive brownstone on Stuyvesant Street in Manhattan's East Village.

"What do you have for me?"

He and Rowan had a deal. He would walk into any meeting with a prospective client, but Rowan gave him a heads-up on who he was dealing with. None of the others who worked at Bryant & Waites had the luxury of a thirty-year friendship with the man who drew up the client profiles and research for Gideon.

"Female, thirty-two, comes from old money, wedding." It was never more than that, because employees didn't talk about the people who walked into the office. Discretion was all-important at Bryant & Waites.

Darcy stretched tall and brushed the seat of his pants. He straightened his tie and slipped on his jacket, which he'd laid carefully over the bench. Rowan bounced up, patting his cheek.

"Looking fine, Mister Darcy."

He stepped away before Darcy could connect to shove Rowan, and then laughing, they fell into step beside each other and made their way from the park to the office, Rowan going in first and taking a seat at the desk in the foyer. That was his kingdom, and he was damned good at controlling everything.

"Ready?" he asked Darcy, who assumed his best serious expression and nodded.

"Always."

Rowan pressed the intercom. "Lieutenant Darcy Bridges is here for you, sir," he announced.

He always did that, added Darcy's rank and surname, making him look good and creating the impression that Darcy was the exact boyfriend-for-hire the client needed. Then he always said he didn't have to do much because who wouldn't want a former army lieutenant who wore a suit well and was the quietly confident type?

Darcy wished he believed in himself as much as his friend did.

"Send him in," Gideon said, his strong voice way too loud in the hush of the hallway.

Darcy waited a moment at the door, pulled his shoulders back, then knocked briskly before entering. He sized up the situation immediately.

The woman sitting in the visitor's chair was slim, her dark hair pulled back in a ponytail. She wore jeans and a T-shirt that was more Target than Armani, and she was glaring at him. He fought the urge to check over his shoulder because he'd never had a potential client glower at him before. He checked his instinct to ask why she was scowling, and offered his hand, which she shook firmly.

"Darcy Bridges," he introduced himself.

"Abby Fitzgerald."

"Take a seat, Darcy," Gideon instructed.

Darcy did as he was told and waited for an explanation about the tension in the office.

He didn't have to wait long.

"This is stupid," Abby began with an exaggerated sigh. "I don't even know why I'm here. I mean, for God's sake, I have a PHD in biochemistry, work twenty-hour days on cures for freaking cancer. Just because I don't have access to my money yet doesn't mean… Jesus… Right?"

She glanced at Darcy, who nodded his encouragement. Normally these initial meetings involved getting straight down to business, but Abby was impassioned, albeit not making a whole lot of sense. She gestured with her hand and forged ahead.

"I'm a determined person who will change the goddamned world, but no, I have to go to a stupid wedding, just to stop my stupid cousin from wrecking everything, defined only by the boyfriend I bring with me."

That was some outburst, and it seemed she wasn't finished, but this time she stood, so Darcy did as well. He would have never let it be said he didn't have manners.

"If I have to hear one more thing from Charlotte about my biological clock, and how ashamed I must be of not having someone in my life, and how she's only doing things for the best, I will go postal on her. Doesn't matter what I think I need to do to stop her…" She shook her head. Darcy had the impression she was hiding something. "My brother isn't bringing a boyfriend, and you know what she said when I told her? She said that didn't count because it wasn't his responsibility to procreate. What. The. Fuck."

Darcy didn't blink. He'd heard every kind of curse word. Abby had fire in her eyes, and he wasn't going to argue with her rage. Then her temper left her, and she slumped back into her chair, so Darcy sat as well.

"Would you like to start at the beginning?" Gideon suggested, and Darcy waited for the entire story to unfold.

Abby checked her watch and sighed noisily, her body language screaming that she'd rather be anywhere else but there.

The intercom crackled. "Sir, I have an Adrian Fitzgerald here for Ms. Abby Fitzgerald."

"Fuck my life," Abby cursed and scrubbed her eyes. They were a very pretty velvet-brown, and for a second Darcy thought she would cry. Only she didn't. Her defenses pulled down over her emotions quicker than he thought possible. She strode to the door, throwing it open and yelling down the corridor. "Get the hell in here, asshole!"

Darcy and Gideon exchanged brief glances; this certainly wasn't how meetings normally went, but they'd roll with whatever happened.

She came back to the desk and dragged another chair over before Darcy could think of helping. He already liked Abby and prided himself on his instinct to sum up character quickly. It seemed to him she was a strong independent individual, and he'd been brought up by a single mom who'd fought tooth and nail for him who was exactly the same. There was nothing wrong with anyone, man or woman, who demanded their rightful place in life.

A man walked into the room, suit, tie, and matching scowl on his face. He and Abby were so alike, and had the same last name, this Adrian had to be related. Possibly the brother. The *gay* brother. Six foot, slim, as dark as his sister, with eyes that flashed with temper.

He filled the room with fire and anger, and Darcy didn't know whether to be turned on or to go on the defensive. Instead, he erred on the side of caution and waited to see what happened.

"This is not how to do it, sis." Adrian ignored Gideon and Darcy and stepped right up into Abby's space.

Darcy tensed, ready to move between them if this brother of hers let his temper fly. He was a foot taller than his sister, with the build of a swimmer, but his hands were clenched, and there was a dangerous feel to him. Slowly, Darcy stood, waiting to see how this played out. He caught Gideon gesturing for him to retake his seat, but Darcy Bridges was not going to back down in the face of a situation where he could help.

"It's the only way to do it," Abby snapped.

Adrian raked a hand through his hair. "It doesn't matter that you'll be at the wedding on your own. Surely someone at work who knows what's at stake could help. You could attend with a friend. If you insist on someone going with you, then there has to be another option. What about Michael? He likes you. You could ask him."

"Michael is a work friend and doesn't know I'm even alive," Abby insisted. "Read what she sent me." She thrust her phone at Adrian.

He seized it from her, and Darcy took a step forward, not liking the way the tension had ramped up in this enclosed space.

Adrian scrolled down the tiny screen, and then, as if a switch had been pressed, every ounce of anger left him in an instant. Instead, compassion flooded his expression, and he instantly pulled Abby into an embrace. For a second, she resisted before wrapping her arms around Adrian and holding tight. For a few moments, the two of them stood in that hug before she stepped back.

"Graham can't do this to you. He can't restrict funding, not now, not when you're this close. We can find the funding—"

"Don't you think I tried? Please don't fight me on this."

Adrian cradled Abby's face and pressed a kiss to her forehead. "What about Mom and Dad?"

"You want me to go to them? Make some kind of bargain where I sell my soul? You know they would have to sell assets, and I can't do that—"

"Okay, sis," Adrian interrupted. "I wouldn't do that either. But a fake boyfriend, how stupid is that?" He looked at Darcy. "No offense, but we don't need you."

"None taken," Darcy said.

Abby gripped Adrian's jacket. "I *do* need him. I have to go, but I need to look stable and the opposite of everything Charlotte thinks I am."

"I don't like it." Adrian rested his hands over hers. "Abby, just because you don't have a partner doesn't mean that you—"

"I know that." Abby sighed. "I want to look normal, professional, all the things they say I'm not."

"Why don't you go directly to Graham?"

"His P.A. says he's busy, he's never there and he doesn't return my calls. But I know it's just that he won't see me. Everything is done through managers. He can't be seen to be spending time with me. You know why."

"Abby, that was one stupid mistake, one stupid date. You didn't even properly kiss him, and hell, he chose Charlotte anyway."

Abby tilted her chin, and the tension in the room shifted again. No longer was she the one defending her position. Now she exuded determination and confidence. "You can't change my mind."

Darcy was curious about what was in the text, but it didn't appear anyone was sharing it. There were people called

Graham and Charlotte, some kind of date and a kiss, and a mention of funding. It all sounded messy.

Adrian turned to Darcy with narrowed eyes. "This is him, then? That soldier you chose from the profiles?"

Darcy was used to being sized up, and he met Adrian's inquisitive gaze head on, watching the verbal interplay.

"I know people will wonder what he sees in me," she bit her lip, "but he's exactly what the family need to see, and when I analyzed all the possible scenarios and players, it was Darcy who fit what I thought would work."

"And if they find out?"

She shrugged. "If they do, then he won't have been doing his job right." She looked pointedly at Darcy.

Darcy remained impassive as he listened to her rationale for why she'd chosen him from the Bryant & Waites portfolio. She might have thought he fit the part, but it wasn't as if he had to decide to take the job as Abby's boyfriend at all. Still, he didn't like being stared at by Adrian as if he were a piece of meat or discussed quite as clinically as this. He crossed his arms over his chest. It appeared Adrian wasn't fazed by him as he attempted to be as intimidating as he could. Darcy thought that, at any minute, he'd be asking for a full medical history.

Instead, Adrian smiled in apology. "Sorry you had to see all that," he said, talking to both Gideon and Darcy.

"It's not a problem, Mr. Fitzgerald," Gideon answered.

"Adrian. Call me Adrian." Then he tugged his sister to the chair before settling in the spare one she'd dragged over. "Let's start again. I assume you can guarantee total discretion."

The mood in the room shifted. From anger and tension to a quiet calm that Darcy appreciated. He sat back in his seat, hoping to hell he wouldn't have to leap up again because it wasn't so good for his knee. Particularly when he'd forgone the brace he sometimes needed to wear.

"Absolute discretion," Gideon assured and set about conducting a correct and very proper consultation.

"And the day after the wedding we need to publicly break up," Abby added.

"Publicly?" That wasn't new. He'd been asked to do that kind of thing before.

Abby nodded. "But respectfully and with great tact."

"I can do that," he said.

When all the boxes had been ticked, Darcy agreed, in principle to a contract for five full days and six nights, plus preliminary exploratory meetings prior to the wedding event to get to know Abby better. Adrian sat quietly, his expression inscrutable, holding his sister's hand. Clearly something in that text he'd read was enough to have him accepting what was happening in the blink of an eye. Darcy would've gone as far as to say that Adrian was getting into the planning, and when they parted and shook hands, Adrian had gone from rabid opposer to willing participant.

He hadn't even meant to check Adrian out, but the siblings were talking to Gideon, and he decided it was safe to examine him more closely. He started at the shoes and worked his way up. Adrian was shorter than him, but had defined muscles, pants that hugged his thighs, and a shirt and jacket that clung to his pecs. He lingered there for a moment before his gaze traveled up to Adrian's face. Adrian was staring right at him with his eyebrows raised. Darcy held his gaze for a moment. He refused to be embarrassed. Then Gideon asked a question about banking details, and the moment of connection was gone.

Adrian didn't call Darcy on the blatant checking out, and he appeared relaxed as he and Abby left the building. But at the last moment, he turned back to look at Darcy, and something passed between them. A spark of attraction, and Darcy found himself confused about the entire experience.

Gideon came to stand beside him, and they watched the siblings take the steps down to the sidewalk and exit stage left.

"That there is some huge can of family-type worms," Gideon murmured.

"We've seen worse. Remember the Hopewell family when they hired four of us?"

Gideon groaned. "That was a completely fucked-up situation."

"With those two, there were definitely things they weren't saying," Darcy said.

"You sure you're up for this?"

Darcy didn't need the money right now since a particularly lucrative contract with a cosmetics heiress in London had him covered for six months, but there was something about Abby Fitzgerald. Maybe it was her strength or her weakness or just the fact that it was Monday and Darcy was bored already.

Or it was something to do with the sexy and enticing Adrian.

It's probably a mix of both.

Adrian was in his head, and that flare of attraction was something he wouldn't mind acting on *after* the booking was finished.

"Absolutely."

"Okay. Rowan will have the paperwork mailed to you. Good luck." Gideon laid one huge hand on Darcy's shoulder and patted him. "And one more thing, stay away from the brother."

Darcy raised an eyebrow at his boss and friend, going for

innocence, as if it had never crossed his mind to explore a little Adrian-time after the contract was done.

Adrian Fitzgerald was fiery, compassionate, loyal to his sister, and had this quirky but sensual smile. Darcy liked his men with those exact qualities. It didn't hurt that he also had sexy come-to-bed brown eyes and a smile that had Darcy heating up under his suit.

Who knew, but this could end up being a lot more than a standard contract after he'd finished his five days with Abby.

It could actually be way more fun.

Chapter Two

ADRIAN STRETCHED HIS LEGS OUT UNDER THE BISTRO TABLE and leaned back in his seat. The sound of the city surrounded him—the rumble of traffic below, an airplane soaring overhead, the distant wail of a siren. The noises were different from those in the small town he had grown accustomed to in the last few years. There, he could hear the birds chirping, his neighbors' children playing in the yard, and the occasional patter of trains passing through. Abby had been at another meeting with the sexy Darcy. Today they'd been working on his time in the army and her work with cancer research. Abby had labeled this the heavy day, but she didn't look tired or overwhelmed.

He wished he was part of the meetings, mostly to keep an eye on everything in this messed-up agreement, but he also wouldn't have minded seeing Tall and Gorgeous again.

The small balcony of his sister's apartment was quite the sun-trap. He closed his eyes and enjoyed the warmth of the sun on his skin. For a moment, it was as if the world had melted away.

He heard the door open and shut, then Abby moving

around the kitchen, and he called out to her when she didn't immediately track him down. "So how'd it go?"

"It was fine."

Adrian opened his eyes as Abby stepped through the open sliding door. She handed him a tall glass of lemonade and sat opposite him.

"Fine, huh?" He ran his finger over the band of condensation on the glass.

"Yes." Abby sat forward. "Fine."

Adrian jerked back as she reached for the sunglasses sitting on top of his head. "Lay off, would you," he said playfully.

Abby was damned capable of handling herself. He knew that. It was just habit to worry about her. She was kind of his hero. The big sister who was driven and strong-willed, but also warm and funny, who had supported him no matter what life had thrown at the pair of them.

"I'm just saying you're going to have to sound a hell of a lot more convincing if you want people to think you're a real couple." He stirred his drink, pushing down the cubes of ice with his straw to watch them bob back to the surface.

The idea of Abby hiring someone to pose as her boyfriend bothered him. It wasn't so much the fact she was doing it as it was the possible fallout of someone discovering the deception. People could be judgmental and cruel, and there was more than one asshole in the family. He didn't want to see his sister exposed and embarrassed.

"Why do you think we have our little meetings? It's to get to know him so we'll feel more comfortable around each other." She held the straw to her lips. "More me than him."

Adrian nodded. "I know." Was she really okay with having to act lovey-dovey with a stranger?

Determination flared in her eyes as if she knew exactly

what Adrian was thinking. "It's going to work. We're going full-couple on their asses because we need to convince Graham that he shouldn't cut my funding. And to screw Charlotte and the lot of them."

Adrian didn't understand exactly what Charlotte's problem was. As a woman, how could Charlotte look down on another for having success in a world dominated by men?

People are weird. He cast his gaze over his sister, over the pale floral-print dress she wore. He noted her hair was down, instead of in the normal ponytail, and how it fell in non-natural curls over her shoulders, and the fact she was wearing makeup. It was strange to see her like that. He'd been sure her wardrobe was made up of iterations of the same two outfits—the blouses, tailored jackets, and pants she wore under her white lab coat at work, and jeans and T-shirts for her downtime.

Abby dropped her shoulders, and for a moment, Adrian thought Abby's conviction had wavered. "Yeah, screw 'em," he said. He would do anything in his power to support her.

"Darcy will play his part, and I'll play mine." She met Adrian's eyes. "You too."

Part of the plan had to involve someone who knew of Darcy's existence, so it didn't seem he had appeared from nowhere.

Which he has.

"Of course, but..." He sighed. "What if people ask lots of questions? The whole point of what Charlotte said to you is that you're married to your work, and all of a sudden—*poof*—here's a boyfriend. Don't you think she'll be suspicious?"

"She'll be too busy fawning over Imogen, the epitome of womanhood and exquisite bride, to care about me." Abby pursed her lips. There it was again, that hint of doubt.

Not so convincing, Sis.

"So long as you have your stories straight, I'm sure it'll be fine."

"Exactly. Which is why I want you to come to the next meeting with Darcy. It'll be the last time I see him before the wedding."

"Me? Really?"

She gave him a firm look.

Adrian let out a breath. "Okay fine." He wasn't exactly comfortable with the whole situation, but meeting Darcy again would probably help put his mind at ease. After all, it wasn't as if Darcy hadn't done this before.

"This'll work. I mean, he's ex-Army. He'll be able to handle anything unexpected and not break under interrogation. Not even from Mom."

"So that's why you chose him."

"Of course." Abby crossed her legs and smoothed the folds of her dress. "Well, that, and you know I have a thing for beards."

Beard. Humorously appropriate given the situation.

"It is a great beard." *I have a thing for beards too, the soft touch of them on my inner thighs…*

"Isn't it?" Abby flashed her teeth as she smiled.

"Well groomed."

Abby nodded. "Right?" She snorted a laugh, then cleared her throat. "We'll be fine."

Adrian stared down at his drink. He pictured the Darcy he'd met briefly at the Bryant & Waites office. There had been this calm but scary aura about him, and the look in his eyes bore a hefty weight that, under normal circumstances, Adrian might have crumpled beneath. But not then, not where his sister was concerned. He pictured again how Darcy had been out of his seat as if he were ready to defend Abby in an instant.

I'm glad.

If Abby was set on doing the whole fake boyfriend thing, then it seemed she'd picked well when selecting Darcy.

Doesn't hurt that he's hot too.

Adrian pursed his lips and rested his head in his hand. Darcy Bridges, ex-Army, the full tall, dark, and handsome package, and, for a fee, he would play the role of Prince Charming for a day, a night, a week.

I should hire him. That would never happen. *As if I could.*

He was convinced Darcy had checked him out with a long, deliberate rake of his piercing gaze that stopped briefly on his chest and the slyest of smiles when their eyes had met. He definitely had an interest in Adrian that was more than just friendly.

When it came to men, Adrian had a patchy history of bad luck and heartbreak. He'd had his confidence shaken too many times. He considered the worst of his exes—the one who'd cheated, the other one who'd stolen from him, and the last one who'd made Adrian feel like shit for not being the *right* kind of gay man he could love.

Maybe Abby's got the right idea. It wasn't as though she'd never dated anyone. Her priorities just lay with her scientific work.

Adrian put his glass on the table. "Have you thought about what I said? You know? About Mom and Dad?" He hated lying to his parents. He hated lies, period.

"They don't need to know."

"Sis."

"Have you seen Mom try to lie? Do you remember when you asked her if Santa Claus was real?"

Adrian shrugged. "Not really. No."

"It was bad. Really bad. She went all red and flustered. It's better to get a real reaction when she meets my *boyfriend* for the first time. Besides, I want her to enjoy the day. Justin is her and Dad's nephew, and unlike us, she actually likes him and wants to go to the wedding."

Justin, the groom, had a questionable personality and had played to the typical image of a spoiled rich kid any time they'd hung out when they were young and into their late teens. It wasn't that Justin was all bad, but he seemed to enjoy feeling important and being on top, the best. If he saw a weakness in someone, he was quick to exploit it. His competitive streak was a mile wide.

Probably why he followed his daddy into law.

"I do like Justin," Adrian said. Abby snorted, clearly unconvinced, and Adrian couldn't help laughing. "Maybe it's not the way Mom acts you should worry about."

The single reason he had accepted the invitation to the wedding in the first place was for his parents' sake. He had probably only been invited out of obligation and in the name of *family*.

"It's not like I'm his biggest fan either. Not after some of the crap he pulled when we were kids."

"Kids say and do dumb stuff." Adrian ran his fingers over his earlobe, twisting his piercing. "He didn't mean it."

Adrian had been a small child, slim, zero athleticism, and happier joining his sister playing house than running around with toy guns. In his early teens, he'd started taking up some sports in an attempt to build muscle, and it wasn't until later that he hit his growth spurt and filled out a little. His mind went back to Darcy and the strength that had radiated from him. He and Justin the jock would probably get along.

"I should have punched him."

Adrian sighed. His sister had been a force to be reckoned with as a child. "Because that would have helped."

"I guess not," Abby said. "I'm hungry." She glanced over her shoulder.

"Nice try. You're really not going to tell them?"

Abby pulled a strange face and made a strained sound.

"What if Mom gets the wrong idea?"

Abby pursed her lips. "Isn't that the point? She's *supposed* to get the wrong idea."

"I mean her thinking you've seen the light and that weddings and grandchildren are on the agenda. You know she sees you as her only hope." He picked up his drink. "What if she takes up quilting? Knitting? Not so subtly leaves wedding magazines out on the coffee table every time you visit?" He sucked on his straw and side-eyed Abby.

"Damn it."

"I'm not saying you have to tell her."

"I know. But your point is a valid one." She tapped her fingers against her glass. "Gah. I'll think about it."

"And quite apart from the fact that you would forever be in Mom's debt, have you thought about approaching the 'rents for access to the money you'll inherit?"

"That was the first thing I thought of. I mean after I realized that I would owe Mom so many favors. But you know that the entire estate is tied up in land. There's nothing they can do."

He and Abby were the land-rich cash-poor side of the family, but there had to be some resources they could get to in an emergency. Of course, an emergency was a new car or a vacation, not millions in funding for a research project. No, Abby needed the support of their cousin's husband's pharmaceutical empire. Shame the cousin in question was Charlotte, who was fiercely possessive of her husband and hated that he and Abby had once shared a kiss.

A kiss that had gone nowhere, but Charlotte was one of those cousins you could never be friends with.

Adrian smiled and decided they needed to change the subject. "Then I would like to propose a toast to the beautiful couple." He raised his glass in her direction. "In the words of a wise woman I know 'it'll be fine.' To Darcy and Abby." He raised his glass in her direction. "To Dabby."

Abby chuckled and knocked her glass against Adrian's. "Dabby."

May you pull this off, sis.

ADRIAN LIGHTLY GRIPPED the handle of the coffee cup and twisted it back and forth. Did he really need to be here? Today was Abby's final chance to meet with Darcy before the wedding, and though he had agreed to it, Adrian didn't really get why he was there. It wasn't essential for him to know the finer details or the plot summary of their fictitious first meeting.

He lifted his cell phone off the table and checked the time when the screen lit up.

Fashionably late as always.

Abby was dedicated to her work, but sometimes it was as if she forgot the rest of the world existed beyond a petri dish.

Like coffee dates with your brother.

He smiled to himself. He wouldn't change her for anything.

"Adrian."

Adrian raised his eyes, spotting his sister. Abby was leading Darcy by the hand, confidently strolling in Adrian's direction. Her hair was tied back, and she wore jeans, a baby blue tank top, and short brown jacket.

The dresses didn't last long.

Abby waved and flashed a bright smile. Behind her, Darcy was gazing over at the menu boards above the counter. His head bobbed, and he laughed as Abby picked up the pace and dragged him along with her.

What is this feeling?

Adrian clenched his hand beneath the table.

They look good together.

There was an ache in his chest.

I'm jealous.

"Hey, you." Abby released Darcy's hand when she reached Adrian. With a smile, she wrapped her arms around his neck and planted a firm kiss on his cheek. "You remember Darcy?"

"Nice to see you again." Darcy leaned slightly as he offered his hand.

"You too," Adrian said.

Darcy gripped Adrian's hand in a firm but brief shake, then sat down facing him.

Abby rested her hand on Darcy's shoulder. "A latte, right?"

"Please."

"Ade, do you want anything else?"

Adrian shook his head. "I'm good. Thanks."

"Okay. Back soon."

Adrian curled his fingers. The sensation of Darcy's hand in his lingered.

Jealousy. He had never felt that before. Not where Abby was concerned.

It's all pretend. The feeling was irrational. He should be happy Abby was able to be so carefree and relaxed around Darcy. That was the only way her plan was going to go through without a hitch.

"Were you waiting long?"

Adrian cleared his throat and met Darcy's gaze. His eyes were a deep shade of brown, almost black, were fixed on Adrian, and he felt the same overwhelming strength in Darcy as he had back at the company office.

"No. Five minutes, maybe." *More like twenty.*

"Your sister's quite the character," Darcy said.

Adrian looked over to where Abby was standing in line. "Yeah." He pursed his lips. "She'll be okay, right?"

"In what way?"

"She won't end up hurt. You'll do your job properly." Adrian stared at his sister's back. Guilt crept through the length of his spine as he remembered all the crap Abby was dealing with because of family members. How could he have been jealous of her and this fake boyfriend thing?

Darcy sat forward and rested his folded arms on the table. "I don't know all the reasons behind what's going on, but I can promise you I will do everything I can to make the week a success. That's my job, and I do my job well."

Adrian faced Darcy and feared he might buckle under the intensity of his gaze. He was so gorgeous, all chiseled good looks and utter determination written on his face. After a moment's pause his expression softened.

"You don't have to worry." Darcy's voice was low and steady, comforting.

"Her white knight." Adrian ran his finger up and down the side of his cup.

Darcy shrugged and leaned back. "I don't think she needs one, but if that's what she wants me to be, then that's what I'll be."

Adrian gave a short nod. "Thank you." He met Darcy's eyes again and found himself lost in their sincerity. Darcy believed what he was saying, and in turn, Adrian believed him, believed *in* him.

Is this…? He gripped the top of his thigh. The jealousy he'd felt made way for something worse, the warmth of desire.

"Everything okay?"

Adrian blinked when he heard his sister's voice. "What? Yes."

Abby took the seat beside Darcy. "They'll bring them over." She pulled her chair closer to the table. "What did I miss?"

Adrian didn't know what to say.

"Your little brother here was just telling me about your terrible personality." Darcy grinned at Adrian.

There was no getting away from the fact Darcy was an attractive man, but his smile, the focus in his eyes in that moment were enough to make Adrian catch his breath.

Longing. Desire. Attraction.

What the hell am I thinking?

Abby patted Adrian's arm. "Aw. Thanks, bro."

Adrian laughed it off. "Someone had to warn him." He stared down at his coffee, Abby and Darcy's conversation blending into the general chatter of the coffee shop. He raised his head as Abby shyly ducked hers and laughed at whatever Darcy was saying.

It's just pretend.

Chapter Three

DARCY LOVED THAT ONE OF THE PERKS OF THESE assignments were the hotels that were a long way removed from a tent in a battle zone. Abby had rented a suite, and it was gorgeous. But it was also the first problem Darcy had identified, however luxurious it was.

"Won't people think it's weird you rented a suite?" He'd been expecting to share a room and had had plenty of practice at sleeping on a sofa bed.

"I'll tell anyone who asks that I need the second room for my work." She crossed her arms over her chest, and he'd noticed that defensive posture before. "They won't care as soon as I start dishing out chemical reactions and talking about placebos and test groups."

"Which one do you want?" The suite was two bedrooms, a large sitting room, and a balcony overlooking the pool.

"I'm not worried." She waved in their direction, then opened her phone and stared at the screen. "You choose."

He checked them out. One of them had an attached bathroom with a whirlpool bath, the other was a more standard setup and slightly smaller. He took that one and hoped to hell she used the bath. She was so tense. Maybe soaking in a tub would help her get rid some of the tension she permanently carried around with her. It was as if the moment she'd stepped into the car, she'd become a different person. Brittle, stressed, and as if she'd put up a shield to everyone.

Well, except for her brother. He was clearly someone she trusted, and he wondered what had happened to her to make her so brittle. The meetings they'd had so far had gone smoothly, but by far, the one that had been the biggest success was when Adrian had been there as well. The others had been more structured, ticking the boxes of things she wanted him to know.

Childhood pet, Fluffy, a white cat, died when she was ten.

Boyfriend, James, lasted from grade ten until twelve when he told her that science was boring.

Guy at work who was what Darcy would call a lab partner. Name, Michael. Abby's eyes lit up when she spoke about him.

House, no. Apartment, yes. A sprawling place with two rooms converted into study space.

They'd had one of the meetings at her place, and with a keen eye, he'd noted the absolute pristine layout of her study rooms contrasting with the barely controlled chaos that filled the rest of her home. She'd told him to look around, opened her closet, and asked him to choose things for the week they were away.

Evidently, she thought *escort* meant a man with an in-built fashion sense. She'd clearly missed the fact he was an ex-soldier. Her closet was filled with more of the kinds of things he'd already seen her wear. No long dresses, no purses, two pairs of fancy shoes. Though she had been unenthused with him for pointing out the obvious lack of clothes suitable for a high-class wedding venue, she had gone out of her way to acquire a dress for their next meeting. Just the one.

It was clear she had loathed the whole experience of browsing racks, fitting rooms, and the attention of boutique sales assistants, and it was then Darcy had realized this was an emergency even he couldn't handle. The solution? She'd given him all her measurements, and he'd passed them on.

Rowan confirmed that the agency had been allocated a budget and that they'd taken care of things. Apparently.

There was no sign of bags yet, but he was sure that Rowan would have them delivered soon.

"This is yours." He gestured to her room, and she nodded.

"This is stupid," she snapped, powered off her phone, and tossed it onto the sofa. "I'm out of the office two hours, and already they've messed up today's tests."

Her fingers crept to her throat, and then she pressed one hand to her chest, her breathing quickening. He stepped toward her, wanting to do something to calm her down, but she stopped him, pushed her shoulders back, and pasted a smile on her face.

"Show me my room, then," she said.

They were just inside when Darcy had to divert to answer a knock on the door. A bellhop with three large suitcases had arrived, along with Adrian, who hovered behind him.

"Your bags, sir," the bellhop announced and wheeled them in, taking the tip that Darcy offered before leaving.

Adrian came in as he left. "Where's Abby?"

"In her room."

Adrian shot him a glance and nodded. "She's stressed, isn't she?"

Darcy considered his answer carefully. He was here as Abby's partner, to be her barrier against the world, to stop the nonsense she was subjugated to. He should tell Adrian everything was fine, but this was her brother, standing there all sexy in a suit and with compassion on his face.

"She's unsettled."

"I'll go in." Adrian knocked, then walked straight into her room, and Darcy heard low laughter and talking. They were so close, the two of them, and he envied that a little, not having any siblings of his own.

He checked the first label of the suitcases the bellhop had arrived with. One was his; the other two were from the Bryant & Waites agency, for Abby. He took his into the bedroom he'd called and unpacked everything: three suits, one monkey suit, jeans, shirts so soft he wanted to sleep in them, and all the right underwear with the correct designer labels. Not that anyone would see those, but as Gideon always said that the person a man pretended to be started from bare skin up.

By the time he was back out in the main room, the two cases had vanished, and he assumed Abby and Adrian were unpacking, and sauntered in to check out what they'd been sent. Abby was nowhere near the case. It was Adrian doing the unpacking, holding up each dress as he hung them in the closet.

"I won't wear that." Abby was mutinous when she looked up from her phone. "Can you imagine me wearing that?"

Adrian shook a black dress, pretty much the same as a million other black dresses, and then hung it up. "You will, and you'll look beautiful. Won't she, Darcy?" Adrian stared at him expectantly and waited for an answer.

Darcy had learned his share of things after three years of working for Bryant & Waites. He knew all about how to act with company who could buy and sell him a thousand times over, how to make a cover story work. He knew a lot of things, just not so much with the dress thing.

"It's beautiful and perfect for the wedding," he said with feeling.

Abby raised an eyebrow. "Maybe you should wear it then."

"I meant on you," Darcy corrected and winked at her.

She laughed and sat in the chair by the window, which framed the ocean views in dark wood.

"You can go, boys; both of you. I need to work."

Adrian huffed and eyed the expansive desk in the corner of the room. "You said you wouldn't work this week."

She sank lower in her chair. "Ade, I'm here for designated social interactions where Graham will also attend. You knew I was lying when I said I wouldn't work."

He pressed a kiss to her head and then backed out the room, tugging Darcy with him. "Let's go."

In the main room, they stared at each other, and Darcy felt as if he should be saying something inspiring, suggest they get a beer, or at least starting some kind of random conversation.

"Come on," Adrian said. "We need to talk."

"What about?"

Adrian sounded deadly serious, and for a moment, Darcy felt certain that he was about to be told Abby was an ax murderer or something.

"Abby suggested that we are upfront with you, all covered by the privacy clause, okay?"

"Absolutely."

"I know damn well Abby hasn't told you anything near what you need to know."

Darcy was puzzled by that assessment. After all, he and Abby had covered a lot. He didn't get time to ask for more details when Adrian left, so he grabbed his room card and phone and placed them in opposite pockets. Then he followed

Adrian out of the room onto the huge landing area, surrounded by large pots filled with plants and what he guessed was some kind of signature color for the wedding, given that everything he'd seen so far had been canary yellow. Bright flowers, wall hangings, yellow bunting. Enough to burn his eyeballs.

Who said that people with money had any sense?

Adrian called the elevator, an old-style thing with a gate and an internal door, decorated in an art deco style that had to have been added as an afterthought to the older mansion.

"I was here for a wedding before Christmas. It's a lovely place. My room is right there." He pointed to a door farther down the corridor. "Suite 73."

He had a suite as well. Was he sharing it with someone? A boyfriend maybe?

"That's a lot of space for one man," Darcy observed and immediately regretted it when Adrian frowned.

"I was supposed to be bringing—never mind, I like the space."

He was clearly going to say something else about a boyfriend, maybe? Darcy wanted to shake the information out of him, only because he needed to know.

Why do you need to know? Keep your mind on the job.

They stepped out of the elevator into reception, and Adrian bypassed the people queuing for registration, his head bent, and seemed to only breathe when they'd made it outside. He didn't talk even then, striding away from the hotel, around the side, down twenty stone steps, and across the wide lawns. When they reached the edge and it seemed as if they were going to walk over, they came to solid fencing and the sharp fall of cliffs beyond. The ocean was calm, but Darcy loved the whisper of the waves as they curled onto the beach. The scent of salt was on the breeze, and he inhaled, then braced two hands on the fence and stared out toward the horizon.

"Where do I start?" Adrian pondered, but it was a rhetorical question as he then launched into an explanation. "Did she tell you about Charlotte-call-me-Charlie-McBitch? Our cousin with the attitude, who is a mess of jealousy and pride, who decided at a young age that Abby was fair game at any and all family events?"

"Charlotte Lenham, née Fitzgerald, first cousin, younger sister of Justin "the ass" bridegroom. Yep. We covered her and her husband, Graham, pharmaceutical multimillionaire, who from photos, appears to have about twenty years on Charlotte. They make an odd couple, but on further investigation, he has a lot of money." He kept his tone even, and Adrian snorted a laugh.

"They really seem to love each other," he said. Then he pointed back at the large mansion they'd walked from. "Look at that place."

Wait, weren't they about to talk about Charlotte the cousin? Why was Adrian changing the subject already?

Darcy turned with his back to the fence and looked up at the grand place that had once been the summer home for a rich family. It was impressive, with a huge middle section with wings that curved down each side, dramatic towers, and so many windows reflecting the sunlight that the building seemed to glow with a light of its own.

Darcy had done his research. The forty-seven-bedroom *Heathers* was one of the grandest of Newport's summer cottages, built by the immensely wealthy McDonald family back in the late eighteen hundreds. It stood right next to *Breakers*, which was larger, but then *Breakers* had been built by the Vanderbilt family. Unlike the other mansions that were open to the public, *Heathers* had been bought by an oil tycoon in the seventies who kept it like it used to be. The brochures said it had been sympathetically restored and was available for rent as a wedding venue. The cost had to be huge, and as expected, the service had been impeccable.

He'd read all that online, but only standing here did he get a real sense of just how much money went into a place like this, and how much of an act he'd have to put on for the next five days.

"It's impressive," Darcy commented and waited for more because Adrian clearly had things to get off his chest.

"In that place is the bridegroom, Justin. He's a good guy. Mostly. He's a bit of an idiot but a nice guy really. He's older than me, if you recall, closer to Abby's age. Then there's Imogen, the bride-to-be. I like Imogen, and she and Justin are good together. This will be a good match and will hopefully last the course, as much as I can predict anything for sure." He paused.

What did any of this have to do with telling him Abby's story?

"But?" Darcy prompted.

"Look, the reason I'm telling you this is that Abby isn't here for the wedding, not really."

"I kind of got that from her already."

"Yeah, well, she and Justin were close for a while as kids. He has brains as well, went to Harvard, studied law. But even the chance of talking to him doesn't get her to go to a family event like this. She doesn't suffer fools gladly, and well over half our family is all about money and society and all the crap that goes with it."

"You're part of the family."

Adrian glanced at him with a rueful smile. "I'm one of the normal ones," he murmured. "If you count normal as not really having to work and having everything handed to me on a platter."

"That's not true. Abby told me you work for the family in finance?"

"That much *is* true, but I didn't *have* to work to get the appointment."

"Tell me more about Abby?" Darcy willed him to continue, not wanting to hover over Adrian's role in the world. What he needed about Abby was more real actionable intel than he'd had from her or the sketchy dossier that Rowan had prepared for him.

"Yeah, Abby, well, that brings me to our cousin, Charlotte. I genuinely don't know what happened to her. She's not a bright person, but she's hard-nosed, determined, focused on the future. She married Graham Lenham when she was twenty-one. He's from a big pharmaceutical family. He's fifteen years older than her, totally besotted, a really nice guy, down-to-earth, and he loves talking shop with Abby, much to Charlotte's disgust. But…"

He kicked at the dirt and sighed noisily, as if the grass had personally upset him. Then he continued, and this time, he sounded angry.

"Graham and Abby had a thing, a long time before he met Charlotte. It was more of a meeting of the minds than lust, and it was no more than one kiss, and they became friends. It's Graham's money that is funding the majority of Abby's research, and Charlotte seems to have this whole insecure thing going on. Where she thinks at any moment Graham would go running off with Abby."

He paused then and looked at the sky.

"As soon as invites went out for the family wedding of the year, Charlotte began to text Abby. Nothing too bad at the start. Saying how nice it would be to chat. Then moving onto what Abby would be wearing and how she was sure there would be other singles at the wedding who would be *alone* like Abby."

"Abby doesn't strike me as someone who would worry about that."

"She isn't, but then the last text came in. Up to that point, Charlotte had been really subtle, warning Abby away from the wedding. But this last one was right in Abby's face. How Graham had considered withdrawing funding. I saw the text, and there was no room for misinterpretation. She was telling Abby, no more money from her husband."

That was a big part of the puzzle Abby had become to Darcy. He'd questioned why she would even come to the wedding in the first place.

"I'm confused."

Adrian sighed. "The message went on about how Graham was concerned about the suitability of Abby continuing in her role. Charlotte implied that if he didn't see Abby at the wedding, he might not think about her and go ahead with canceling her funding."

"So, wait, Charlotte was doing her a favor? Giving her a heads-up?" That didn't seem likely; otherwise why would Adrian be standing there explaining things to him?

"No, you see, we know Charlotte, and she pushed the warning too far. She was all sickeningly sweet, sent private messages, with photos of the dresses she'd bought, and the jewelry she had, and implied that Abby wouldn't want to come to the wedding anyway. That to her and Graham, she was a lonely spinster who probably needed to stay at home."

"Okay, so Charlotte *really* didn't want Abby here."

"Yep, and that was the wrong thing to do, fuck with Abby's job and funding. Hence, Abby's infuriatingly stubborn determination to be here. She wants to talk to

Graham one-on-one and ask him face-to-face why he's removing funding."

"Noted. Arrange for Abby to talk to Graham. Ignore Charlotte."

Adrian bumped elbows with him, and they exchanged smiles, then stood in companionable silence for a time, facing Heathers, the old lady looking beautiful bathed in the afternoon light of the June Sunday. The first event of the week was a welcome supper, champagne and canapés on the east lawn at seven p.m., and he guessed at some point they'd need to make a move back inside, but right now it was nice to get some fresh air. He could smell Adrian's cologne, a subtle scent that tickled his senses. He wondered where the scent would be concentrated, at his throat maybe, or down on his chest, right near his nipples. It wouldn't take much to walk farther away from the hotel, and he could find out.

"Why do you do this?" Adrian asked, interrupting his daydream. It was a question that inevitably came up, whatever his role was, and one that Darcy had rehearsed the answer to.

"Honorable discharge from the Army, and a friend of a friend said he had work for me. I didn't want to work security or go back to school. Hell I didn't know what I wanted to do. This was supposed to be a one-off gig, but I kept getting jobs, and it pays for the other things I want to do in my private time." He used a harder tone at the end, just to stop Adrian asking what those *things* were because he wasn't going to share every part of his private life with people he was working for. Not that it was earth shattering; charity work with a dog sanctuary, and some security work at a local school. Still, it was his private life, and Adrian didn't ask.

"You ready for tonight?"

"Ready as I'll ever be."

"Is there anything I need to go over with you?"

"No, I find the simpler, the better in situations like this."

"What does your *partner* think of you doing this?"

When Darcy glanced at Adrian, he could see the calculation in his beautiful dark eyes and the slight twitch of his mouth, as if he'd already guessed all of Darcy's secrets.

"Single right now," he said, "but it's my job, so *he*'d have to accept it."

Adrian held out a hand to shake, and Darcy took it immediately. "Thank you," he murmured.

His grip was firm, and Darcy didn't want to let go. This was bad. He needed to stop, but Adrian's touch was warm and strong.

Adrian nodded and didn't continue that line of questioning. "We should get ready. Let's go back up to our rooms the long way to avoid everyone."

"Avoid them? We'll be meeting everyone in a few hours, anyway."

"Well, yeah, but I need the time to steel myself for pinched cheeks and comments about where my boyfriend is and questions about which of the *gay* shows on television I watch."

When they got back to their floor, having used the kitchen entrance and the back stairs, the door to Abby's room was shut. Adrian went into his suite, and Darcy felt that maybe he should make sure Abby was okay. He went to knock, but there was a note tacked to the wood.

Yes, I know the time. No, I don't really want to go. Yes, I can dress myself. No, you don't have to remind me when it's time to go. The note had a tiny *A* at the bottom, and he couldn't help but smile at that. She had a personality that he was enjoying getting to know.

Just like her brother.

Chapter Four

SHOULD I HAVE TOLD HIM EVERYTHING SO CLINICALLY?

Adrian sat on the end of the bed. He felt guilty for laying everything on Darcy, but he'd had to do it. Darcy needed to understand why he was here and what was at stake for Abby.

Damn it.

He lay back and closed his eyes, wishing he could stay in his room all evening.

Would I get away with staying in here?

As tempting as the idea was, it wasn't fair to his sister or their parents.

I'm here now anyway. I might as well get this wedding crap over and done with.

Opening his eyes, he let out a sigh. He didn't know how Abby was feeling right about now, but the stress tightened his chest. Worrying wasn't going to help anyone. He knew that. The last thing he wanted was for Abby to be influenced by how he was doing and maybe end up feeling even worse than she already did. He needed to relax and try to enjoy himself. Put his faith in Darcy.

Also, he needed to stop *thinking* about Darcy in an inappropriate way.

I need to get changed.

With a grunt, he pushed himself back up. He rubbed his eyes, then stared through the open double doors to the sitting room. It really was a lot of space for just him. He'd had plenty of time to fix the reservation, maybe get a smaller room, and yet he hadn't. He and Austin had separate rooms to retire to when they stayed away together. Austin had always said personal space was healthy and that not every couple had to sleep in the same bed.

I should have known.

The suite had been the last thread of hope tying him to his broken relationship. It had been over for months. He'd been kidding himself.

I want to fall asleep in a man's arms. I want to sleep with them in the same freaking bed.

He closed his eyes, pictured a single blue thread that was his former lover, and then…

Snip.

ADRIAN PLAYED with his small hoop piercing as he waited for the elevator. He blew out a heavy breath and lowered his hand, pushing it into the pocket of his pants.

It's going to be fine.

With a *ding* and clatter, the doors slid open.

Seriously?

As his eyes met Charlotte's, it was as if he'd had the wind knocked out of him.

She smiled as she tightened her hold on her husband's arm. "Adrian," she said.

He stepped inside. "Charlotte." Adrian forced a smile,

quickly turning his gaze to Graham. "Evening, Graham." He tensed as Charlotte leaned toward him and bopped him on the nose, long scarlet nails a flash way too close to his eyes.

"Call me Charlie, silly."

Adrian nodded. "Sorry, I forgot. It's been a while."

Not long enough.

The doors jerked shut.

"Aunt Vi's seventieth birthday celebration, wasn't it?" As usual, Graham's tone was pleasant, his expression warm.

"Oh yes. Good memory, honey," Charlotte said. She fluttered her eyelashes and hugged herself to her husband.

He and Graham shook hands. "I'm so sorry that Abby couldn't make it," Graham said and sounded really regretful.

"Sorry?" Adrian was distracted by Charlotte's plunging neckline, which left nothing to the imagination. He didn't know why she dressed like that. She was a pretty girl, but somehow she'd decided using her body was a good thing.

"Charlotte said your sister wouldn't be here."

Adrian feigned confusion. "She's here, in a suite on the same floor as I am."

Something passed over Charlotte's face, shock maybe, and Graham glanced at his wife and wore a concerned expression. He didn't have time to get involved in whatever happened five years ago, but it was wrong for Graham to avoid Abby as he did.

He could nip everything in the bud and ask Graham outright about funding, but now wasn't the time, and it wasn't his place. Abby had it on her to do list. All Adrian had to do was watch for any catfights that broke out, with his cousin Charlotte at the center of it all.

I want to go home.

The elevator came to a standstill. Then the doors parted,

and Adrian opened the gate. Voices echoed down the corridor.

"After you," Adrian said, taking a step to the side.

"We'll catch up later," Charlotte murmured, but it sounded like a threat. She lifted the skirt of her dress slightly as she stepped out of the elevator.

Adrian hesitated, in the hope of putting a few steps between them. Charlotte's heels tapped on the polished tile floor, and reluctantly, Adrian followed. He tried to maintain a distance, slowing his pace so he didn't catch up to the couple.

"Ade." He glanced over his shoulder, noticing Abby and Darcy heading in his direction from the elevators. He stopped. If Charlotte had heard Abby's voice, she didn't turn around.

Adrian took a few steps back in the direction he'd come. "You made it."

"Don't act so surprised." She hit his shoulder with the black clutch bag she was holding. "What do you think?" she asked of her outfit. "I channeled my inner Charlotte."

Abby wore a red evening dress and looked nothing like Charlotte at all. Its empire line accentuated her bust, and the skirt came down just below her knees, hemmed with lace matching its half-length sleeves. She'd pulled her hair back into a bun, with a large black flower clipped at the back of her head, which matched her other black accessories. She was beautiful and not at all desperate to get attention as Charlotte clearly was.

"Charlie," Adrian corrected her dryly. "Not Charlotte."

Abby raised an eyebrow.

Adrian shook his head. "Elevator fun. Don't ask."

"Oh." Realization dawned on Abby. "Oh. You saw her?" She bit her lip and frowned. "Was Graham with her?"

"Yeah, he looked shocked when I said you were here, and she went pale."

Abby breathed in deeply. "Whatever. If he wants to tell me he's stopping the funding for the lab, then he can tell me to my face. And it's too early in the week to let anything get to me." She wrapped her hand around Darcy's. "Darcy, I would like to apologize in advance for any family crap you are subjected to or have to witness."

Seemingly unfazed, Darcy raised their hands and pressed a kiss to the back of Abby's. "It's not them I'm here for." His voice, those words were deeper and sexier than they had any right to be.

Adrian swallowed hard and checked out the floor. He was aware of the slight flush in his sister's cheeks, the strengthening of her resolve, and surge of confidence in her stance.

And the fact that his throat tightened and his libido perked up.

Darcy is quite the hero.

He lifted his head, his breath hitching when he found Darcy staring at him. His gaze was as dark and intense as ever and penetrated Adrian, straight to his heart.

This is bad.

Lustful thoughts about his sister's hot fake boyfriend were not supposed to be on the agenda for the week.

Get a grip.

Darcy's admission when Adrian had asked about a partner had left Adrian longing for things he shouldn't, plus it didn't help that Darcy looked damn good that evening. Dark dress pants hugged him in all the right places. A black shirt open at the throat teased dark chest hair Adrian dreamed of running his fingers through, set off by a tan-colored jacket.

"Ready?" Darcy asked His smile was effortless, and he gently swung his and Abby's arms, offering his support.

"Definitely. I need to talk to Graham. Convince him to… yeah, ready."

Darcy leaned in, this time pressing a kiss to her cheek. "Remember, relax." He took a step, tugging at Abby's hand to encourage her to walk by his side.

Adrian followed. He studied Darcy's back, from the lines of his body beneath his buttoned, fitted jacket to the slight limp. He wondered what that was about and resolved to add it to the list of things he wanted to know. Eventually, he settled his gaze over Darcy's shoulder, aware that being caught staring at his sister's boyfriend's butt would garner more attention than he needed.

"Good evening." A young woman stood at the entrance to the reception room. She wore her short, blonde hair swept back from her face, was dressed in a smart waiter's outfit of black dress pants and waistcoat, and held a silver tray of champagne flutes. "Please help yourself to a glass. There is orange juice available to the left as you enter if you'd prefer something nonalcoholic."

"Alcohol sounds great," Abby said and helped herself to a glass.

Darcy also took one and turned around. "Champagne?" He offered it to Adrian.

"Sure. Thanks." He took the drink.

"We hope you enjoy your stay." The waitress ducked her head slightly, then stepped back.

"Should I leave you two alone?" Adrian asked as the room opened up. He was sure there was somewhere he could hide out.

Abby put her hand on his arm. "Don't be silly. We might need you."

"For what?"

"A diversion while we make our escape." Abby chuckled.

Adrian sighed. "Thanks, Sis." He sipped the champagne.

What he thought was a single room was actually a series of connecting lounges. A collection of mismatched period sofas, armchairs, and stools were grouped together around low tables. They were covered in an array of patterns mostly accented in burgundy and gold.

"Fancy," Darcy said. He raised the glass to his mouth and tipped back his head, downing most of his drink. "Do you know all these people?"

Abby scanned the room. "Some. Not really familiar with anyone from Imogen's side."

"We met her parents, didn't we?" Adrian said.

"We did?"

Adrian stared at his sister. "I think so." He pursed his lips. "Maybe it was at one of those family things you blew off for work."

"Ah. Probably."

Adrian laughed. Abby didn't even care.

"Can you see Graham anywhere?"

Adrian checked out the room or at least the bits they could see. He could've been behind any of a number of huge marble pillars adorning the grand space.

"Guys." Darcy cleared his throat. "There's a lady trying really hard to get your attention." He indicated over Adrian's shoulder.

Abby stood on tiptoes, arching her neck. "Oh, crap."

Darcy frowned. "Who is she?"

"She…is our mother," Adrian told him.

"Paula," Darcy stated.

"Okay, so we're going to have to go over there," Abby

said in a strained voice too low for anyone but those standing beside her to hear. She waved at their mother.

In the end, Abby had decided not to tell their parents the truth. Adrian wasn't sure he'd agreed with Abby, but then it wasn't his future being toyed with.

Abby linked her arm in Darcy's. "We just downplay everything. Don't give her any silly ideas that we're super serious about each other." She pinched the material of Adrian's jacket. "You're coming, too."

"Yes, Sis." It wasn't as if he was going to stand there alone. That was more embarrassing than third-wheeling the pair of them.

Adrian led the way. "Mom." He raised his hand in a small wave.

"Adrian," said Paula. She stood and pulled him into a brief hug. "Looking handsome as always." She kissed him.

"Where's Dad?" When he leaned back, she rubbed his cheek.

"Lipstick," she said. "He's with your uncle. Probably talking stocks and shares." She looked past him at Abby. "Abigail."

Abby flashed a smile. "Mom."

"Let me look at you." Paula took Abby by the hand and checked her up and down. "You should wear dresses more often." Her gaze shifted to Darcy. "You must be Darcy."

Darcy held out his hand. "Paula, lovely to meet you."

Paula frowned at his hand, then shook her head. "Don't be so formal. Any *friend* of Abigail's is a friend of ours." Before Darcy had a chance to react, Paula wrapped her arms around him in a hug. "Oh, don't you smell nice."

Did Abby warn him Mom's a hugger?

"It's wonderful you're both here. I'm so glad you managed to unshackle Abigail from that desk of hers."

"Mom."

"It's true. I hardly ever see her, and she never tells me anything." Paula side-eyed Abby.

"Abby works hard. She's very good at what she does." Darcy's tone was calm but firm, and the expression on his face as he stared at Abby was one of pride and support.

Wow. If he hadn't known better, Adrian would have been convinced right then and there that Darcy cared for Abby. *The doting boyfriend.*

Relief. Pride. Jealousy. Loneliness. Conflicting emotions overwhelmed him.

I need a minute.

With a sigh, Adrian eyed the empty wine glass on the table. Excusing himself to the bar seemed a good idea. "Does anyone want a drink?"

Without hesitation, Paula said, "I'll have a white wine. I don't remember what your father said it was called, but a medium-dry." Her cheeks were already a little flushed.

Mom and wine. Were any of them ready for that?

"I'll have one of those too. A large glass for me." Abby patted Darcy's arm. "Darcy will give you a hand, won't you, Darcy?"

There was something in Darcy's expression when his gaze met Adrian's, an uncertainty. Did he realize Adrian had been trying to run away? "Sure. If you want."

"Really, I'll be fine. You should stay here."

"It's not a problem, is it, Darcy? He'll go with you." Abby widened her eyes as she met Adrian's gaze.

Okay. Okay. Hint taken, Sis. He figured Abby wanted a moment to reaffirm their Mom on exactly how uncommitted she and Darcy were to one another.

"No. No problem at all," Darcy said as Abby released his arm.

Adrian cleared his throat. This was for Abby. "Then yeah. Thank you." He turned around. "We'll be back soon." He couldn't bring himself to say anything else to Darcy, not until they reached the bar and Darcy spoke to him.

"Sorry about that. Your sister really wanted me out of there." Darcy stood next to him and rested his arm on the side of the bar.

Adrian shook his head. "It's fine."

"If you want some space, I can take their drinks to them and say you're using the restroom or you've run into someone and catching up."

Adrian turned his head slightly. Sincerity shone in Darcy's eyes, and he truly appeared regretful at having been ordered to accompany Adrian. "Don't worry about it. I just get uncomfortable around all *this*." He glanced around the lounge. "Doesn't matter how many social events or family celebrations I attend, I never seem to get used to it."

"I guess it's not for everyone." Darcy scanned the room. "It kind of fascinates me."

Adrian pressed his lips together.

Money. Privilege. Extravagance. Being a Fitzgerald was supposed to be a blessing. He had wanted for nothing and yet…

I'm being slowly suffocated.

After rejoining Abby, they managed to go a whole fifteen minutes before they came upon Charlotte and Graham, but it was with Charlotte leaving and Graham supporting her solicitously.

"So sorry we can't catch up," she simpered, clinging to her husband's arm. "I just need to lie down."

"Graham, can we talk?" Abby asked.

Graham flashed her a pointed look, but Charlotte coughed to clear her throat and took her husband's attention.

Graham reached out his other hand to touch Abby's arm. "Absolutely. We have so much to discuss—"

"Graham," Charlotte snapped. "I need to lie down."

Charlotte stared at him. She was pale. Maybe she *was* ill. Who knew? But that put an end to the conversation as she deftly guided Graham in the direction of the elevators.

"Shit," Abby muttered. "I need another drink."

"HOW MUCH DID YOU DRINK?" Adrian winced as Abby lifted her arm and caught him in the face with her bag.

"More than three, less than five." She chuckled and tightened her hold on Adrian's neck.

"Nearly there," Darcy said. Abby's other arm was slung over his shoulder.

In a line, they turned, then sat on the end of the bed.

"Made it." Abby let out a dirty laugh and fell back onto the mattress.

Adrian rested his hand on her knee. "Yes, we did."

"So you're officially a lightweight." Darcy yawned.

"They were big glasses." Abby put her arms above her head and smacked her lips. "He didn't want to talk to me. He's scared of me. So I had *big* glasses…"

Darcy rubbed his brow. "Okay. Time for bed." He reached down and grabbed Abby's leg by her ankle, raising it to slip off her shoe. He tossed the black heel toward the dresser, then did the same for her other foot.

"You're not going to undress her, are you?" Adrian looked down at his sister. Her eyes were closed, and her lips parted with every sleepy puffed breath.

"No. Are you?" Darcy said in a hushed voice. He stood.

"No."

Darcy carefully removed the flower from Abby's hair, then put it and her bag on the nightstand. "Give me a hand."

Between them, they positioned Abby higher up the bed. Darcy grabbed a blanket from the closet and lay it over her. He pulled his hands back when Abby muttered and rolled over.

Adrian couldn't keep his eyes off him. Darcy was so tender, so caring. Was that all an act too? Part of the service?

"Hey, come on," Darcy whispered. He nodded toward the door as he backed out of the room.

"Thanks for your help." Adrian quietly shut the door behind him.

Darcy slipped off his jacket. "No problem."

Adrian lingered by Abby's bedroom door but couldn't pull his gaze away. The more time he spent with Darcy, the more perfect he seemed. "I should head back to my room."

"You sure? I don't mind if you want to hang around here for a bit." Darcy sat on the sofa. "We could have a drink."

Temptation.

"Thanks. But I should probably go. Rest up for whatever tomorrow's activities are." He edged toward the exit.

Darcy glanced at the floor, then got to his feet. "Sure thing."

Is he disappointed?

"Thank you again. I know Abby's glad to have you here; we both are." He stopped by the door, surprised to find Darcy already there, reaching across him for the handle.

So close.

The faint scent of cologne mixed with the smell of alcohol on Darcy's breath.

Darcy cocked his head, holding Adrian's gaze. "Good night." He pushed down the handle.

The temperature outside the room was cooler. Adrian

suddenly felt clearheaded. "Night." He swallowed, noting the heat Darcy radiated as he passed close to him and left the room. He didn't look back but heard the soft click of Darcy shutting the door. Releasing his breath, he curled his hand in the front of his shirt.

This is dangerous.

Chapter Five

THERE WERE PLANS. A WHOLE SCHEDULE OF THINGS THAT had been provided for guests, ways of meeting and talking, and chances for Abby to get Graham alone that Darcy was ready to find. The plan that they'd been given invited guests to a buffet breakfast first thing in the morning, followed by luncheon on the lawn, dinner in the blue room. It was one meal after another.

However, there had been no sign of Graham or Charlotte anywhere so far, certainly not at breakfast.

The couple didn't turn up for the guided tour of *Breakers* either. When the time came for luncheon on the lawn, Darcy had been lulled into a false sense of security that maybe Charlotte was trying her hardest to avoid everyone.

Then she showed up in a swirl of white silk, her game face on, and no Graham at her side. She headed straight for Darcy and Abby, with absolute determination on her face. He braced himself for whatever was about to happen and curled his fingers into Abby's. He'd been less apprehensive facing a drill sergeant than having to face down the sour-faced Charlotte.

"Abby, I'm so pleased you came," she lied and pulled Abby close to her.

They were a study in contrasts, Abby all curves, in a simple lilac dress, and Charlotte waif like and dressed in flowing low-cut white.

They embraced, briefly, and then Charlotte stood back.

"And who is your guest?" she asked and held out a hand, which Darcy shook firmly.

"This is my *boyfriend*, Darcy," Abby announced, and Darcy saw an immediate change in Charlotte.

"A boyfriend? How wonderful," she said, and her cautious smile became wider. "Darcy, it's so nice to meet you."

What had just happened? How had she changed so drastically in such a short time? The dynamic changed again when Justin and his bride-to-be joined the small group. They'd met briefly last night but hadn't talked much. Justin seemed fairly normal; the bride, Imogen, level-headed.

They all exchanged hellos and chatted about inconsequential things: the glorious weather, the amazing house, and the wedding itself. He tuned in just as Justin was finishing some story about a friend of his from work who was wanting a date.

"… so I said I had a cousin who'd be interested in a hookup and gave him your number, Adrian."

"What?" Adrian asked. "Why would you do that?"

Justin was confused. "He's gay. You're gay. It's just sex. I don't see a problem."

"So you gave a complete stranger my private number so we could have sex?"

Justin huffed as if he thought Adrian was being completely stupid. "He's not a *complete* stranger, idiot. He's the guy in the mail room, and he's just looking for sex. I mean, that is what you all want, isn't it?"

"By all, you mean gay, right?" Adrian flushed scarlet, and Darcy could see how much effort it took for him not to snap. He tensed, ready to diffuse the situation.

"Could you get me a drink, Adrian?" Abby asked and firmly planted herself between her brother and the idiot cousin. That avoidance tactic worked to get Adrian away, and then silence fell, and it was Imogen's turn to control the conversation.

"Darcy," she began, "Abby mentioned you were a soldier. Where were you posted?"

"Did you see any action?" Justin added.

"I saw enough," he said, and his knee seemed to throb in time with his pounding heart. *No war questions, please.* He called on all his learned tactics to divert attention away from the question, but Abby slipped in and changed the subject smoothly.

"This is a wonderful place for a wedding."

That seemed to work, Justin and Imogen talking weddings, Charlotte smiling like an idiot, and Abby gripping his hand so tight he thought the circulation might be cut off. Thankfully, Adrian arrived with a tray-full of drinks he'd stolen from a passing waiter. After they each took one, he proposed a toast.

"To Justin and Imogen," Adrian announced, and they all raised their glasses.

"You said that the event had been delayed?" Graham slid his way into the circle, his arm going around Charlotte's waist.

"Not this one silly," she said without missing a beat and leaned into him. "The museum tour."

"My mistake," Graham murmured, although he didn't sound entirely convinced. "Abby, could we talk?"

"You don't need to talk to Abby now," Charlotte said. "Stay here with me."

Graham pulled Charlotte close and cradled her face, then spoke low and firm. "We have things to clear up, sweetheart. Okay?"

Charlotte gripped his arm. "What if I don't want you to go with her?"

Graham sighed. "This is work. Just work."

"She has a boyfriend."

He frowned at her. "Charlotte, not now please..." He released her, and she let her hand drop as they parted, pulling back her shoulders, but she seemed as if she was going to cry.

Abby held Darcy's hand tightly and took him with her as she followed Graham. This was it, he guessed, the moment in which Graham revealed he was removing funding. She was tense, and he rubbed his thumb against her skin in reassurance after which she threw him a grateful smile. He glanced back once at Adrian, with his unreadable expression, and then Graham stopped away from the people milling around on the lawns.

"I know this isn't the time or place really," Graham began, "but the Japan setup is taking me away from the US. Louisa said you've been trying to talk to me, but it wasn't important. You have such a good handle on what happening at Lenham Med, I wanted to—"

"We're so close," Abby interrupted desperately, "you have to keep the funding in place to let me finish the work I'm doing there. I know that there isn't money in research, but when you first funded me, you told me about your mom and her cancer, and I know we're close to finding something that will help people like your mom in the future. Whatever happened between us, whatever Charlotte asks you, please, you can't take this away from me."

He frowned and held up a hand. "I think we're talking at cross purposes. Wherever did you get the idea I wasn't going to continue funding you? And what does Charlotte have to do with any of this?"

She opened her mouth and then shut it again, and Darcy knew he had to say something to smooth what could get awkward. After all, that was what he was being paid for.

"I think what Abby means is that she is worried about the industry in general," he said and tightened his grip on Abby's hand momentarily to warn her that he was handling it. He could feel her shaking as if she was waiting for the ax to fall.

Graham shook his head. "I wanted to tell you that I've put safeguards in place guaranteeing secure ring-fenced funding for the next five years."

Silence. No one spoke, and then Abby let out a hitched breath, and Darcy got the impression that Abby would cry over something as important as her work. He pulled her into a sideways hug.

"That's wonderful news, isn't it, darling?"

She clung to Darcy as if her legs were jelly and nodded.

"Thank you," she murmured.

Graham smiled. "So I wanted to discuss the variety, volume, and velocity corresponding to the biomarkers related to mortality. I was utterly fascinated by your last report."

"As you're aware, businesses of all kinds are using big data to guide their decisions," she began.

"Rather than intuition," Graham interjected. "Wait." He went to the nearest waiter and took the entire tray of hors d'oeuvres he was carrying, then hurried back. "Can I borrow your girlfriend?" he asked and offered Darcy and Abby their choice from the tray. Abby took a salmon parcel, but Darcy declined. "I have food, and I'd love to ask you questions about the testing."

"Charlotte won't like it," Abby murmured.

Graham glanced back at the small group, where Charlotte stood watching. He pressed his lips in a tight line.

"Charlotte doesn't like a lot of things recently."

Darcy heard sadness in his words. Something was really wrong with Graham and Charlotte.

"I could stay, Abby?" Darcy asked, quite prepared to jump in if needed, but equally aware that things weren't going as anyone expected. Graham wasn't withdrawing funding, if anything, he was offering more and for a longer period. The relief in her expression was obvious, her frown gone.

"I'll be a little while," she said, already slipping into work mode in her eagerness to talk to Graham.

"I'll be around." He hugged her very quickly for appearances before pressing a kiss to her hair.

She was already gone, talking numbers and theories as the two of them walked away and took a seat on the bench with views of the ocean. So he went back toward the group they'd just left.

"Get used to that," Charlotte said. "Work always comes first. Look at them, thick as thieves." She was fighting tears.

Darcy immediately defended Abby, as he was supposed to. Actually, like he *wanted* to. "Abby's work is vital; it will save lives. I have no issue with her talking to Graham."

Charlotte's eyes narrowed, but the tears vanished, and a mask of coolness slipped into place. "Yes, I suppose, but what about you, now? You're on your own, just like I am. We should go for a walk."

The last thing he wanted was to go for any kind of walk with someone who appeared to be able to turn their emotions on and off like a switch. But before he could think up a suitable excuse, Adrian jumped in.

"Sorry, Charlie," Adrian intervened. "We're signed up for activities this afternoon."

This was news to Darcy, but at that moment he'd have done anything not to have to continue talking to Charlotte who had moved awfully close to him. Still, he rolled with it and followed Adrian away, after inclining his head toward the group.

They got as far as the main door and into the hotel, where Paula was holding court.

"And this is Darcy," she exclaimed loudly, gesturing for him to stop. "He's Abby's *boyfriend.* An Army lieutenant."

Four women, in pearls and silk dresses turned to examine him, with reactions ranging from shock to disbelief.

"Abby has a boyfriend?" one of them asked and was nudged forcefully by the other standing next to her.

Paula smiled benignly. "We knew she wasn't a completely lost cause. That she was just waiting for the right man."

"Maybe now she can settle down and have a family," another of the women said.

Darcy bristled and died inside. This wasn't the first time he'd heard these words from a family he had to fool, but this was *Abby* they were talking about. She was married to her work, and why shouldn't she be? She'd probably change the world, and that had a hell of a lot more value than being some man's arm candy.

"Sorry, Mom, we have to go. We're on a schedule."

Adrian dragged him away before any of the others got to speak to him, and even though Paula pouted, she didn't argue.

They made it out through the foyer and to the elevators.

"That was close," Adrian said when the doors shut on

them. "Last time I got cornered by the coven, I was asked if I was friends with god knows how many gay men they knew, and did we, as a team, have a secret handshake. I'm not joking. They're rejects from fifties sitcoms; it's insane."

"Then thank you for rescuing me."

"What happened with Abby and Graham?" Adrian asked. "I saw her smiling, so it can't be as bad as she thought?"

"All I know is that he had no intention of withdrawing funding." The elevator shuddered but didn't stop, and they got out on their floor.

"So what was Charlotte playing at? Why did she mess with Abby's head like that?"

Darcy waved his key card over the pad to enter his room. "I get the impression that it's more a Graham/Charlotte issue." That was all he was going to say because Adrian was staring at him so intently, and there was concern in his expressive eyes.

"He actually met Charlotte through Abby, and they ended up marrying. So the kiss was clearly nothing to him. I know it didn't mean anything to Abby."

"It might be an insecure thing on Charlotte's side, then." He stepped into the suite.

"Hey, Darcy?" Adrian asked, and Darcy stopped. "We have five hours until dinner. You want to get out of here?"

"What if Abby comes back?"

"She'll be talking work until someone stops her," Adrian said, and there was so much pride in his voice.

"I'm not sure I should leave the hotel in case she needs me."

"C'mon, Darcy, live dangerously."

That was the very definition of dangerous. Spending time with a man he was attracted to, while he should be focusing completely on Abby. That was what he should *not* be doing.

"I shouldn't," he murmured.

"Sorry?"

Darcy sighed inwardly, thinking of all the things that could go wrong, cursing the fact that the one time he actually found someone he wanted to get close to he was on the job. So he should stay in his room, wait for Abby, and not get involved with his client's brother. That included any and all activities or times when they got to talk alone. Adrian was gorgeous, his eyes full of humor, and his lips plump and kissable, and he was *off-limits*. At least until after this event. There was nothing to stop them from meeting up *after*.

"Did you hear me?" Adrian asked, and he was closer this time, right behind Darcy, and it was too close for comfort.

He could walk inside his and Abby's suite, close the door, and not follow his traitorous libido anywhere near Adrian. That would be the safe thing to do.

Only, that wasn't what happened.

"As long as we don't go too far. And give me five to change into jeans," he heard himself say.

What the hell are you doing, Darcy Bridges?

Chapter Six

THIS IS OKAY, RIGHT?

Abby needed time with Graham, and while she was away, Adrian couldn't let Darcy fall into the clutches of Charlotte, the coven, or their mother. He was aware Darcy could fend for himself, but surely there were only so many convincing lies to tell and ways to avoid awkward conversations. One slip and Abby's charade would be over. He wouldn't let that happen.

The week's barely started. We might need to save some of those excuses for another day.

Adrian drummed his fingers on the arm of the sofa as he waited. He was doing this to help Abby. Darcy too. He looked over his shoulder at the door to Darcy's room. The door was ajar. He couldn't clearly see inside, but every now and again the daylight he glimpsed through the gap was interrupted as Darcy passed by.

Out of the goodness of your heart.

After a string of bad romances, Adrian appreciated Darcy's company. Sure, it was probably part of the act. Darcy's kindness had been bought and paid for. But for the few moments when Darcy's attention was solely on him, Adrian swore there was something more to it. A connection. Something real. He pursed his lips. Maybe his intentions weren't entirely honorable in stealing Darcy away from his sister.

I'm selfish.

He turned his head, idly playing with his earlobe.

"Do you need to grab anything from your room? A change of clothes or anything?" Darcy asked.

Adrian lowered his hand as Darcy came to stand in front of him. He shook his head. He was comfortable enough in what he had on—red shirt, gray waistcoat, black skinny jeans, and loafers.

"Okay." Darcy sat beside him and leaned forward to lace his boots. He had changed into a pair of smart jeans and a pale striped shirt. "So what's the plan?"

The plan?

"I don't know. I didn't think that far ahead." He drew a full breath. "I just thought it was better if we avoided certain people for a while."

Darcy laughed. "So I'm in protective custody."

"Playing bodyguards sounds hotter—" Adrian grimaced and quickly got to his feet. *What the hell, Ade?* "Or so I hear. Anyway, shall we go?" He couldn't look at Darcy, choosing to focus on the exit. He needed to get out of that room. It was a spacious suite, and yet, suddenly, it was if it were no larger than a closet. Darcy was close, too close.

For a moment, Adrian managed to trick himself into thinking Darcy hadn't heard him. He realized he had been mistaken when Darcy said, "I thought about bodyguard and security type jobs when I came out of the Army."

Darcy seemed to allow Adrian to put distance between them, holding back from getting off the sofa straight away.

Adrian opened the door. He took a deep breath, put on a smile, then faced him. "But you ended up doing this?"

"I needed a change of pace, I guess." Darcy stood.

"It's definitely a change of pace."

Darcy shrugged. "You'd think, but sometimes I'm not so sure." He grinned. "Danger lurks everywhere."

Adrian quirked an eyebrow. "Seriously?"

"You have no idea. Let's see. I've been bitten by a date's dog. Another time, I got a black eye from someone elbowing me in the face on the dance floor. Then I was covered in scratches after trying to break up a fight between a date and her sister." With each recited instance, Darcy approached the door. "Oh, and then there was the time a date's ex pushed me off a bridge."

"Off a bridge?" Adrian was horrified.

"It was some cutesy arch thing over a stream, nothing major," Darcy said dismissively. "The worst part was that I was sitting up to my waist in cold water, soaked, and she *dumped* me right there and got back with the other guy." Darcy stopped when he reached Adrian. "I knew I'd been hired to say 'screw you' to the ex, but, seriously, I kind of felt hurt." He laughed and met Adrian's eyes.

There it is again. That something *in his dark gaze.*

"Sounds rough." Adrian stepped out into the corridor.

"There's also the time I let the little brother of a date lead me astray." He pulled the door closed.

Adrian swallowed hard. He shouldn't respond, but it was as if he couldn't help himself. "What happened?" There was an unevenness in his voice, and he knew Darcy caught it.

A smile spread across Darcy's face, and he headed for the elevators. "Sorry. Spoilers." He walked backward for a few steps. "Come on. I know where I want to go."

"WHAT ARE YOU DOING?" Darcy stood several yards ahead, his hands on his hips.

"Shut up." Adrian stopped. He was out of breath, sweaty, and his shoes were full of sand. He glanced back at the cliff side and the path they had taken down to the beach. The path they would have to climb back up.

I need to get back in the habit of going to the gym.

"What's wrong? We're having an adventure." Darcy did three jumping jacks, although Adrian noticed he did wince a little on the third one.

"What are you? A puppy?" Darcy had way more energy than Adrian had banked on.

Darcy unbuttoned his collar, then began a slow jog in the direction of the ocean. The way Darcy had talked about the beach and the water, it was as if a fire had been lit inside him.

Adrian couldn't stop himself from smiling as he watched Darcy.

He looks so happy.

His cell phone vibrated in his back pocket. There was a message from Abby in reply to the message he'd sent to her earlier: *Saving your boyfriend. Text when you're done.*

He read her reply—not all that surprised when, after insisting there was no need for them to hurry back, she said she'd be in her room working.

With a sigh, Adrian kicked off his shoes. He picked them up, turning them upside down to get rid of the sand. With his shoes in his hand, he followed Darcy, occasionally breaking into a jog to try and catch up.

"Hear that?" Darcy said when Adrian finally caught him. "No matter what else is going on, that sound, it always makes me feel better."

Adrian stared at the wet sand and wiggled his toes. He couldn't remember the last time he'd been to the coast. He closed his eyes and listened to the ocean, to the *whoosh* of waves rolling up the beach.

"Want to walk in the water?" Darcy nudged Adrian's arm.

Adrian lifted his head and watched the movement of the waves. "I'm fine. But if you want to… I don't mind waiting with your things."

Darcy breathed in deeply and folded his arms across his chest. "I'm happy right here." He stared toward the horizon.

Adrian's stomach fluttered and rolled. He spread his legs to secure his footing. *Why do I feel like I'm falling?* It was the same sensation he had gotten when he was a child and his Dad would speed the car up as they went over a sharp hill.

"Think anybody would miss us if we just stayed here for the week?" Darcy faced Adrian. "We could pitch a tent?"

Adrian looked back up the beach. "Tempting, if I didn't have a ten-thousand-dollar suite to make use of."

Darcy nodded. "I guess."

Adrian raised his free hand to his ear. He didn't know why he suddenly felt guilty. Maybe it was because the aura around Darcy had changed. Darcy appeared sad, and Adrian noticed he was rubbing his knee.

"Are you okay?" he asked and pointed at the knee.

"Old wound, nothing too bad. Anyway, we should probably head back." He turned his back on the water. "And I should check in with Abby."

"She's probably buried in data by now. Spreadsheets and pie charts or something."

"I can see that." Darcy smiled as he stared up at the cliff. "Are you going to manage the climb back up?"

"You mean we aren't radioing for the family helicopter to come get us?"

Darcy furrowed his brow. "Wait, you guys have a helicopter?"

"No." Adrian laughed. "At least I don't think we do."

They started walking back to the cliff.

"Private jet?"

"No."

"Chauffeur?"

"Not me personally, but there are some in the family with chauffeurs and other staff. I know my Aunt Vi has a chef." Adrian shrugged. "Maybe when I get to her age, I'll want someone to cook for me every day, too."

"I love to cook," said Darcy.

"Consider yourself hired," Adrian said and wished he'd kept his mouth shut when Darcy winked at him.

Adrian kicked his feet as they reached the dry, loose sand. He wanted to make a lighthearted joke about résumés and application forms but instead said nothing. He could feel his cheeks heat up as just the thought left him feeling embarrassed.

Silence fell between them, and Adrian struggled to think of something to talk about. "So, I—Ow, ow." He hopped sideways as a sharp pain shot through his heel.

"You okay?" Darcy touched Adrian's elbow and glanced down.

"I think I stepped on something." He lifted his foot behind him. Blood oozed from a cut. "Crap." He hissed and held onto Darcy for balance. "That's just great."

Darcy scanned the ground. "Just stay still." He crouched and moved Adrian's hand to rest it on his back.

With a grimace, Adrian focused on his foot. Blood mixed with sand across his skin.

This is my punishment for getting stupid ideas.

"Looks like the stem of a glass." Darcy carefully held up

the broken piece that looked as if it were from a wine glass or champagne flute. "Some idiot didn't clear up after themselves." He pulled a tissue from his pocket and wrapped it around the shard. "There's a trash can at the bottom of the steps."

Adrian sighed and stared upward. It was a long walk back to the hotel.

"Let me see." Darcy grabbed Adrian's ankle, causing him to wobble. "Hold onto me."

"I am." Adrian pressed his hand to Darcy's shoulder.

"Doesn't look deep."

Heat radiated from Darcy through the material of his shirt, and Adrian distracted himself from the discomfort of his injury by imagining what was hidden beneath. He pictured tanned, broad shoulders and strong arms that would hold him tight, deep colored nipples he would tease to attention, dark chest hair to run his fingers through—

"Ow." Adrian flinched.

"Sorry, but I'm done."

Adrian checked·his foot. "A Band-Aid?"

"You'd be surprised how often they come in handy. A lot of my female dates have a tendency towards wearing ridiculous shoes." Darcy slipped his wallet into his jeans. "I wasn't able to get all the sand off, so it'll need a thorough cleaning when we get back."

Adrian nodded as Darcy lowered his foot. As lovely as the ocean was, he longed for a long soak in the oversized tub in his air-conditioned suite.

"Hop on." Darcy had remained crouched on the sand.

"What?"

"I'll carry you."

Adrian parted his lips.

"You don't have to look so horrified." Darcy looked up at him and smiled. "I don't bite."

"What about your knee?"

"I'm good," Darcy said. "Now get on, or would you rather limp to the top?"

"I guess when you put it that way." He checked the nearby area, back along the beach, then the path up to the hotel It wasn't as if anyone was around to see them. "Sorry if I get sand on you."

Darcy shrugged. "Don't worry about it." He held his arms out behind him, encouraging Adrian to climb on.

We're really doing this. Adrian pulled on his shoes. "Okay. How do we…?" He gripped Darcy's shoulders and pushed up with the balls of his feet. "Oh God," he said as he was hoisted up.

Darcy hooked his hands under Adrian's thighs and jostled him a little higher.

Adrian wrapped his arms around Darcy's neck, trying his hardest not to throttle him as he panicked at the sudden lack of control he felt. "Don't drop me." He crossed his wrists.

"I won't."

The solidity of Darcy's back against his chest eased Adrian's fears. "Thank you."

"Like I said, don't worry about it." He started the long hike back along the series of paths and steps leading back to the hotel. Every so often he stopped and took a breath, but not once did he put Adrian down.

Adrian turned his head, closed his eyes, and briefly rested his cheek on Darcy's shoulder. Darcy smelled good. It was a mix of scents, some because of the heat and the hike down to the beach. There was Darcy's cologne, and then the smells of the ocean carried on the salty sea breeze.

"Are you all right back there?"

"Uh-huh." Adrian lifted his head. Darcy's face was next to his.

Too close.

Neither of them said anything for a while. Adrian stared down at the ocean as Darcy walked higher up the path.

"What food do you like to eat?" Darcy asked.

Adrian blinked. "Food?"

"If someone were to cook for you, what would you want?"

A lump formed in Adrian's throat. *What would I want?* "I don't know."

"There must be something. For me, pasta. Kind of boring, I know, but I love the stuff."

"It's not boring." Adrian pressed his lips together tightly as pain throbbed in his foot. "Tomato soup and bread."

"Soup?" Darcy shifted his hold.

"Grandma Fitzgerald used to make it if we got sick when we were kids."

His senses were filled with the memories of those times, of the smells of freshly made soup and baked bread, of the warming taste, of his grandmother's smile as she teased about a secret ingredient. It had been the best kind of comfort food, still was, though these days it was store bought.

"I'm sorry."

Adrian tilted his head, catching Darcy's gaze. "For what?"

"From my notes. She died, right?"

"Yeah. But it was a long time ago. I was in high school."

The two of them became quiet again. Adrian noted the low mumble of voices from above them.

We're already here?

"Stop," he said.

"Why?" Darcy did stop.

"I hear people. Put me down." He patted Darcy's shoulder.

Darcy turned his head so he was able to look at Adrian properly. "Don't be silly. I don't mind."

Adrian opened his eyes wider and said in a hushed voice, "No. I don't want anyone to see us like this. What would they think?"

"That Abby's boyfriend is a great guy? You really think they will see anything else here?" Darcy furrowed his brow.

Adrian wanted to say no one would notice. Or comment. But he knew his family. There were members of the larger Fitzgerald family who didn't approve of him, talked behind his back, pitied his parents for having been dealt such a terrible hand and having a son like him. His immediate family was who mattered, and they loved him.

But this isn't about me. This is about Abby.

"Please put me down," he said.

He didn't know who was up there talking. It might have been total strangers, tourists, but he couldn't take the chance, and he wasn't in the mood to deal with whispers and curious stares.

"Okay." Darcy bent down until Adrian's feet touched the ground.

Adrian stepped back but was unbalanced as his foot twisted at a strange angle.

"Hey." In a flash, Darcy was standing and turned around, able to catch Adrian by the wrist.

Adrian limped slightly as he got used to putting pressure on his injured foot. It hurt, but not too much. Darcy had said the cut wasn't deep, so a clean dressing and rest, and he should be okay. He swallowed as he realized Darcy had moved his hand to his.

Darcy squeezed his fingers around Adrian's and tugged

him under an overhang in the cliff, hidden from everyone. "I've got you." He met Adrian's eyes, seemed to get closer and then—

What is this?

Adrian's breath hitched as Darcy kissed him. The kiss was gentle, brief, unexpected.

Wanted.

Darcy pulled back, but not by much. He held Adrian's gaze. Was he as shocked as Adrian at the kiss? He didn't say anything, simply continued to hold onto Adrian's hand.

"I just had to. I don't know why. This is so unprofessional. What am I doing?" Darcy sounded confused, angry at himself, even lost.

Emotion swelled inside Adrian, and it was as if his ability to think rationally shorted out. He pressed his hand to Darcy's chest, leaned in, and this time it was him kissing Darcy. He closed his eyes, pressed his lips firmly to Darcy's, and lost himself in the man in front of him.

I'm an idiot.

He opened his eyes when Darcy cupped his jaw and created distance between them. "No," he murmured.

Adrian pulled his hand away and pushed past Darcy.

He didn't look back, even when he heard Darcy call his name and was glad when the path looped round and opened up onto the lawns. He halted, surprised to find Abby sitting on one of the patios with their parents. She was probably desperate to escape. They had most likely grabbed her before she could get away after talking to Graham.

"Ade." She called and waved him over. "Darcy."

Adrian glanced over his shoulder as Darcy emerged through the rose arch that led to the cliff path. He sighed as Darcy plastered on a smile and waved back at Abby. "I need to get cleaned up."

"Do you want me to come with you?" Darcy asked quietly so no one else would hear. He worried his lip. He probably wanted to talk about what just happened or to say no to Adrian again. Even though Adrian knew he was being stupid and didn't need to be told no. Abby was so lost among the family all talking at her, and she was why they were doing this.

"No," he said shortly.

"But your foot—"

"I can take care of it myself." Adrian tensed his jaw. "Can you please go and do what Abby is paying you to do. Your job." He knew he sounded rude, but he had to put a wall between him and his foolish attraction to Darcy. The man had been paid to be there for Abby, not for him.

Darcy stiffened. "I know what my job is," he said through gritted teeth and walked past Adrian in the direction of the patio.

Adrian waved at Abby, then pointed up to the hotel. "I'll see you later." Abby frowned. Darcy could explain about his foot for him.

I need some time alone and to think.

It was only the first day, and he was already messing things up.

Chapter Seven

DARCY REFUSED TO CHECK BACK TO SEE IF ADRIAN WAS STILL standing there. His entire focus was on Abby, who smiled gratefully as he moved closer. She stood immediately, and for a moment, Darcy thought they would get away with going for a walk or something well away from the parents. Not that he couldn't handle parents. He wasn't lying when he'd snapped at Adrian that he knew his job. Now he just had to shake off his heated reaction to Abby's brother and slip back into his boyfriend persona.

"Darcy, come sit. We haven't had a proper introduction," Paula insisted. "Harvey, this is Darcy. Darcy, this is my husband, Harvey."

Harvey didn't look up, clearly lost in whatever he was reading.

Abby went straight into avoidance mode. "Mom, Darcy doesn't want to be interrogated."

"Pfft, I won't interrogate."

"You asked the last boyfriend I introduced you to what his life goals were."

"That's a reasonable question to ask of anyone dating my

daughter, don't you agree, Harvey?" This time the use of her husband's name was louder.

He looked up at the strident mention his name, cast a vague smile. "Absolutely, dear." He directed a nod as way of greeting at Darcy, then went back to reading his paper.

Despite the hefty weight of business and money that came with the Fitzgerald name, Harvey seemed one of the more down-to-earth members of the family. He was calm, reserved, a man of few words—or at least that was how he came across. It had become apparent last night, in the brief moment Darcy had spent in his company that Harvey was happiest when his wife was able to shine and take the spotlight. Despite his apparent indifference, love had brightened Harvey's expression as he had watched Paula indulge excitedly in conversation.

"Mom, we were going to junior prom."

Paula pursed her lips. "And doesn't that tell you something? We've not met a single one of your boyfriends since you were at middle school. Ridiculous. Both of you sit down, have some tea. You don't want to go, do you, Darcy?" Paula stared at him in innocence, but a thread of steel ran through her words. She'd painted him into a corner with that unanswerable question. Abby muttered something, but he sat in the chair next to her and took her hand, tugging her to sit.

"There," Paula said, "tell me a little about yourself, Darcy."

He poured iced tea for Abby, topped up Paula's, and then got some for himself. Walking on the beach, *kissing Adrian,* was thirsty work.

He sat back in the chair. "What would you like to know?" He didn't take Abby's hand again, remembering her direction that he shouldn't make it appear as if they'd last as a couple.

Paula regarded him carefully. "Well, we know you're a former soldier, a man of rank."

"Man and boy," he answered. "I hoped to be active for a long time, but I was injured overseas." He didn't go into details, and she didn't ask.

"So tell me, how did you two meet?"

Abby groaned and covered her eyes, and he couldn't help but smile. They had a detailed backstory they'd worked on, but she had made it so convoluted when she'd created it, layers of meetings, building a slow attraction, and he'd argued at the time it wasn't all necessary.

"I'll take this," Darcy said.

Abby shot him a look of relief.

"We met at a coffee shop a couple of months back, not far from Abby's apartment, not that she drinks coffee, but she has a thing for the bagels there, and well, I was there for the coffee. We got talking, and the rest is history."

She stared at him accusingly then, but she stayed quiet, probably eager to leave.

"Do you have any family, Darcy?"

He answered all the questions thrown at him, even the one about his intentions toward Abby to which he gave the pre-agreed answer.

"It's early days."

She nodded, but he must have passed some kind of test because she relaxed into her chair and sipped her iced tea.

"Maybe there is a wedding in my future." Paula was all innocence, but it was a cue for Abby to leap to her feet and grab Darcy's hand.

"We're out of here, Mom," she announced, and he went along with it, holding her hand, exchanging goodbyes, and then allowing himself to be dragged away.

"I think that went well," he said when they were out of hearing range.

"You missed out the bits we talked about. You know, the story of the cat that ran in front of the car and how your friend knew my friend, and—"

He pulled her to a stop and pressed a finger to her lips. "Your mom isn't stupid. Simple is best."

Then he hugged her, still in full view of her mom, and when they separated, she caught his hand against her and smiled up at him.

"You're good," she said.

Arm in arm, they walked around the side of the hotel, only separating when they were out of sight, and then he stopped her.

"I have an hour, and then it's some guy thing with the groom in the bar, with whiskey."

"You're going to that?"

"Need to fit in." He shrugged. *And I want to talk to Adrian, make sure everything is okay.* "But we could go and explore the coast a little? Or go back to the suite, pretend we've gone for a walk, and you could check in with work."

Her smile widened.

"I do need to get hold of Michael. His team has data for me."

Without spoken agreement, they went into the hotel and straight to the suite. Abby holed herself up in her room as soon as they got there. Last he saw, she had her laptop on and papers spread around her. He heard her on the phone, and she was laughing, and it sounded nice. No one could say what another person's happy place was. For Abby, it was chemical reactions, tests, data, and from the way her laughter was low and flirty, it seemed she liked talking to whoever this Michael was.

After a short time, she closed her door, and he killed time until the whiskey tasting in the bar.

As he went to the elevator, he saw Adrian coming out of his suite. He was in different clothes, and he wasn't limping, so that was a good thing. He was probably heading for the whiskey tasting same as him.

"How's the foot?" he asked when Adrian spotted him.

Adrian sighed noisily, turned back to his door, and went into his room. Darcy waited a full minute before he realized that Adrian was not coming back out. There was no way he'd join in with whiskey and bullshit when he'd only said he'd go because he thought he'd have a chance to talk to Adrian.

So he returned to the suite, took a shower, and lay on the bed with a book and attempted to forget that he felt guilty and angry and off-center where Adrian was concerned. He'd known attraction before, but this was different. This was a new kind of desperation, and he had to get the fuck over it.

From his window, he could see the ocean. The book held his attention between bouts of staring, and all too soon, his alarm went off to remind him there was an hour to go before tonight's event, a formal dinner with speeches, apparently.

He couldn't understand why a wedding had to last an entire week, let alone why there had to be so many speeches. But it was his job to get Abby to the event, so he knocked on her door. "One hour, Abby," he called.

She shouted something back, and at a loss of what to do with his time when he felt cranky and out of sorts, he called Rowan to check in.

Not that the guys out on a job needed to do that. Not that he had anything to say, but Rowan was his oldest friend and never failed to make him smile.

"Darcy, is everything okay?" Rowan asked immediately, concern lacing his voice.

"Yeah, I'm just touching base." He kept his tone light, as if he had nothing burning in his chest desperate to get out.

"Shit," Rowan said, and then the call was muffled, and when he came back, the tone of his voice was different, and he was clearly standing in a room with a door or maybe a closet. "What did you do? Oh fuck, you banged the brother didn't you?"

"What? No, *Jesus*, Rowan, I'm not stupid."

"I knew this would happen the minute he walked into the damn room. What the hell—"

"Rowan, I haven't *banged* Adrian."

Rowan sighed noisily. "But you're on the damn phone to tell me you want to, right? God dammit, Darcy, tell me I'm wrong."

"You're wrong. I'm on the job. Why is everyone telling me I don't know my own job?"

"What? Who else told you that? Wait, I need to sit down."

"In my defense, I didn't kiss him much, not really, but there we were on the beach, and he was hurt, and I took him under this outcrop so we could talk some more, and—"

"Stop. I don't want to know. Do we need to do any damage control here?"

He meant with Gideon Bryant. The owner of Bryant & Waites wasn't that cool with the guys he placed going outside the authority they'd been given. It was why he liked hiring anyone who'd been in uniform, told all new recruits he didn't appreciate anyone wandering off-target. That was what Darcy had signed up for, but then Adrian was *right there.*

"No, I stopped it, stopped myself. He told me I needed to remember my role, and stalked off."

"Did he even want you kissing him?" Rowan asked, and Darcy heard the worry in his friend's tone. It wouldn't be Darcy who faced Gideon; it would be Rowan who smoothed the waters because it had been he who'd referred Darcy and backed him. Of course Darcy had proved himself an asset, worked every booking the right way, up until today when he'd stolen that stupid, irresponsible kiss. And now Adrian was avoiding him, which was going to make the rest of the week awkward and messy.

"Darcy? Are you still there?"

Darcy shook the memory of the kiss and the resulting anger away. It hadn't meant anything, just a moment of madness in this structured week of pretense.

"I'm here."

"You know your role there. Support Abby—"

"I know—"

"And wait until after this contract is done to kiss the brother again. Promise me, D?"

That was what he'd phoned to hear. He needed someone to remind him of things. Not about his role here or his responsibilities or what he'd been paid for in particular, but that maybe, after the week was done, he could meet up with Adrian and get the man out of his system.

"I promise," he said.

"Okay then, call me. Anytime. Right?"

"Always."

Call ended, he styled his hair as best he could and dressed in suit pants and a pale-blue shirt, knotting the silver tie in front of the mirror and slipping into his dark shoes. He only had to pull on his jacket, and he was ready for whatever the night threw at him, and there was still an entire thirty minutes left until the event.

Maybe he should go and knock on his door, demand Adrian to listen to an apology. Maybe they could laugh about it all and the fact that Adrian had kissed him back and he'd pushed him away. *I'm so stupid.* He was about to leave when Abby called him from her room.

He knocked and cautiously opened her door. She stood in her underwear, staring at two dresses laid out on the bed.

"Which one?" she asked. "I want to blend in with everyone, not stand out." She poked the one on the left. "And this is scarlet. Everyone will see me and want to talk to me. To us." Then she lifted the other one and held it up against her. "This one, it's black. I like black, but look at this." She thrust it at him, and he took it before she dropped it to the floor. It was perfectly nice.

"What's wrong with it?"

Abby huffed and flicked the material, revealing the thigh-high split when the material parted. "What's the phrase, mutton dressed as lamb?" She seemed sad, a little lost, and at that moment he could see Adrian in her expression.

"Abby, there is nothing about you that makes me think you will ever look like you aren't the most beautiful woman in the room."

She lifted her chin. "You're paid to say that."

He rolled his eyes and removed the black dress from the hanger, smoothing it down and then offering it for her to step into. She did, although she winced as if each touch of the material burned. He held her hair and pushed it out of the way and zipped her up. Then he manhandled her gently to face the full-length mirror.

"Beautiful," he repeated. "Can you see that?"

She met his eyes, then checked her reflection. After a short pause, she moved to the left and glanced at her back as best she could. Then she took an experimental step to see how much of her leg showed. Finally, she shot him a small smile.

"I guess."

"Michael would love you in this dress," he said.

"What? Michael who?"

"Michael, the guy you call at work."

"No. Wait, he won't, we don't, he..." She went scarlet and disappeared into the bathroom. He expected her to stay in there, already thinking of the words he would use to encourage her back out when the door flew back open.

"He doesn't even notice I'm there," she said, hands on her hips, her tone angry. "We're each as bad as the other one, so much to do, so many theories and tests, and we stand together all day, and I think I like him, but I can't say, and he never says a thing. He'd take one look at me in this and wouldn't even react, then start talking equations." Her words were running together, and she'd gone from angry to confused in the space of one small speech.

"I bet he does notice," Darcy said. "I know if I was—"

"Don't say it," she warned.

"What?"

"Don't say that if you were straight, you'd notice me."

Now she was smiling, and he resolved to mention this Michael to Adrian, see if maybe her brother could get the two of them seeing each other out of lab coats.

If Adrian was talking to him.

If Darcy hadn't completely fucked things up.

THE SPEECHES WERE INTERMINABLY BORING. Long, rambling discourses about the groom and his love of snakes, and the bride and her love of spiders. At least that was what Darcy thought the speeches were about. They were full of in-jokes from friends, and he had his hands full with a table of cackling women teasing him and Abby: Paula and her coven.

The group was determined to embarrass Darcy, Abby, and

themselves. Wine was involved, but luckily there was a space between him and them.

An empty chair. Adrian's place.

He hadn't made an appearance, and Darcy went from concerned about vague things like gangrene in his foot to being pissed that the idiot was hiding from his family or from him.

The dinner ended a little before ten, and there was dancing after, but Abby didn't want to dance or stay or have anything to do with anyone.

"Michael has more data," she explained with a smile.

Darcy didn't like to point out that she was smiling at using his name, and escorted her back to her room. When she went in and closeted herself away, he felt restless and needed to get out for air. The urge to knock on Adrian's door was strong. What if the idiot really was hurt? Like seriously enough for Darcy to have to do something?

In the end, he didn't. He fought the instinct to find out and went out for a walk, down the cliffs, along the beach, a long circular path, until he was back at the hotel and it was nearly midnight. There were a few people in the lounge area, and he bypassed them and went through the back corridor.

"...spend time with her and not me!"

"You're being ridiculous, Charlie."

He heard the arguing before he rounded the corner and stopped in his tracks.

"It's not ridiculous when you won't even come to bed with me. I bet you'd go with Abby. I bet she could have a baby. She can do everything else."

"Please." The second voice belonged to Graham. "I didn't return a single one of her calls, in case you thought I was cheating on you. This is ridiculous. We need to talk. I love you."

Sobs followed Graham's plea, and Darcy felt like the worst kind of voyeur. He turned to leave, only to be followed by the rapid click of high heels.

"Wait!" Charlie called, and he guessed she was talking to him. He didn't want to get involved in this, and he took his time turning to face her. She looked like she'd spent hours crying, her mascara trailing down her face, her skin blotchy. "What are you doing here?" she snapped.

He wasn't sure how to answer that one. He was in a hotel, walking in a public place. He had every right to be there.

"Charlie?" Graham rounded the corner and stopped when he saw Darcy.

Charlie glanced from him to Darcy, and then, as if someone had pulled a switch, she threw herself at Darcy, wrapping her hands around his neck and dragging him down for a kiss. They separated before Darcy had a chance to disentangle himself, and she turned and faced her husband who looked like his world had ended.

"Can you see what it's like?" she demanded of Graham, and he stared at her, and hell, he seemed as if he was going to cry as well.

Time for this soldier to leave an obviously private battle.

He strode toward the elevator, pulled the gate, and pressed the button, willing the doors to shut. A second grew into more, and it was the longest few moments of his life until finally the doors shut and the elevator moved upward.

Being dumped into a stream was one thing. He'd also been punched, proposed to, and kissed by a lot of women, but being used as some kind of bargaining chip in a marital fight was one of the rarer occurrences. He wiped his mouth and saw the scarlet on his hand. That had been some kind of wet, sloppy kiss and given with a lot of self-hate. Not like the other kiss he'd had today, which had him thinking about Adrian again.

We need to talk.

Which was how he found himself at Adrian's room, knocking loudly and waiting for him to open up.

They were not going to spend the week avoiding each other. Darcy owed the man an apology, and Adrian was damn well going to accept it. He'd better come out quick before Darcy broke down the door.

Chapter Eight

HE'S NOT GIVING UP.

Adrian rubbed his brow.

"Adrian, you there?" Darcy knocked again.

Why was Darcy being so persistent? Adrian had thought Abby's string of texts, asking where he was and if he was all right was annoying and embarrassing. He appreciated her looking out for him, but he was starting to feel like her kid, not her brother.

There was another burst of short but loud bangs. "Open up."

But this was another level of irritating. Was there anyone in the neighboring suites who knew him?

"Okay, you win," Adrian muttered. Huffing a breath, he got off the sofa, wrapped the hotel bathrobe wore tightly around him, and marched over to the door. He yanked it open and met Darcy's wide eyes.

"Hi—"

Adrian raised his finger, shushing Darcy. He checked the corridor in both directions, wrapped his hand in the front of

Darcy's shirt, and dragged him into the suite. "What are you doing?"

"Choking." Darcy hooked his fingers in the front of his collar and moved it from side to side. He stepped farther into the room.

With a sigh, Adrian closed the door. He hesitated, watched Darcy. "Where's Abby?"

"In her room. Working. But that was over an hour ago. She might have gone to bed."

"It depends on what she was working on. She can lose herself in it for hours, forget to eat, sleep." He folded his arms across his chest and, keeping his distance, walked around Darcy to sit on the sofa. "She's kind of ridiculous that way."

The atmosphere in the room was anything but relaxing, and Adrian wanted Darcy to hurry up and say what he had to say and leave already.

"Did I wake you?" Darcy eyed the robe Adrian was wearing.

Adrian raised an eyebrow. "All that banging and now you care if I was sleeping?" He rearranged the bottom of the robe to cover his knees.

Darcy glanced at the floor.

"Don't worry, I wasn't. I don't know about my neighbors, though."

"Sorry."

"Whatever." Tiredness made him ache.

Darcy sat beside him. "Don't be like that."

"Like what?" Adrian stared at Darcy. "It's been a long day. It's late. I'm tired. I'm achy."

"How's your foot?" Darcy seemed a bit passive, in sharp contrast to the determined knocking of only moments before. "I was worried when you skipped out on dinner. You missed some really...*great*...speeches."

Adrian crossed his legs and angled his foot. "It's fine. Like you said the cut wasn't deep."

"You made sure you cleaned it properly?"

"Yes, Mom." He pressed his mouth into a line. "It's fine, honestly." He lowered his foot. "If that's what you came for, now you know."

"It wasn't. Okay, it might have been part of it but…" Darcy ran his tongue around his teeth. "It wasn't just your foot I wanted to make sure was all right."

Adrian's gaze drifted from Darcy's eyes to his lips.

"It was you and about what happened earlier—"

"Is that lipstick?"

Darcy touched his mouth. "Oh, that."

"It is." Adrian bit down on his lower lip at the pang of jealousy in his chest. "So you and Abby…" A kiss was bound to happen eventually if they were going to pull off the charade of being a couple.

Then why does it hurt?

Darcy wiped at his mouth. "No, not Abby."

The shade was a deep red. Darker than anything Adrian had seen Abby wear.

Jealousy made way for anger.

"Then who?"

"I got caught up in something…awkward."

Adrian frowned. "That's not much of an answer."

"I know. But I'm not sure what I should say. There are clearly issues there, and me spreading gossip isn't going to help." Darcy pursed his lips. "Even if she is a cow."

"Wait. Charlotte?" That was the obvious answer. Adrian shook his head. "Actually, no. I don't need to know." He didn't go in for family drama. He closed his eyes. Why did he feel like he'd been here a week already? It was day friggin' one.

"So, about before."

Adrian opened his eyes. "What about it? You made it perfectly clear how you feel."

"I don't think I did." Darcy edged closer, and Adrian panicked.

"You said no." Was Darcy doing this to mess with him? He went to get up but was quickly pulled back onto the sofa when Darcy grabbed him by his wrist.

Confusion ran rampant through Adrian's head. What was going on? "You. Said. No." He winced from surprise rather than pain as Darcy gripped him more tightly. "No means no, right?"

Darcy relaxed his hold a little and stroked slow circles over Adrian's palm with his thumb. His touch caused a chill to pass over Adrian. He slipped his hand lower, linked his fingers with Adrian's. "I didn't mean no." His eyes drew Adrian in.

"Then—" Adrian's breath hitched as Darcy knelt up. What was Darcy doing?

Darcy tilted his head, gently brushed back Adrian's hair above his ear. "I meant not now. Not here. But…" He came closer, leaned into the space beside Adrian's head. "Don't get me wrong. I want to. Really want to." Darcy's voice was gravelly, and Adrian could feel his heated, alcohol-laced breath on his ear as he spoke. "To do more than just kiss you."

Desire shot straight to Adrian's groin, and he swallowed back the groan that caught in his throat as his erection pressed against the material of his briefs.

"But I won't." Darcy sat back and released Adrian's hand.

"You're cruel," Adrian whispered.

"Five days."

Adrian frowned. "What?"

"Saturday at noon is when we check out of this place and when the contract between me and Abby comes to an end. So five days and then I'll do whatever you want me to do. A drink, a date, a kiss, a fuck. Whatever you want."

Adrian parted his lips. What was he supposed to say? "You're serious?"

Darcy stood. "I think we both feel there's something here, right? If you agree, then I'd like to explore that." He shrugged. "Maybe it goes nowhere, but then again, maybe it does."

Maybe he was tired, but Adrian struggled to believe Darcy wasn't just doing this to toy with him. Darcy must have noticed Adrian was conflicted when suddenly there he was right in front of him, close enough to—

Adrian blinked as Darcy brought up his hand and clamped it over Adrian's mouth. He mumbled into Darcy's palm, wanting to ask what he was doing. He got his answer when Darcy smiled, then leaned forward, pressing a kiss to the back of his own hand.

"I'm serious. About you, us, but also my job." Darcy lowered his hand and backed away. "Nothing is going to happen between us, not while we're here."

He really is serious.

"So, five days. Deal?"

Adrian rested his hand on his stomach as it tumbled from a mix of fear and anticipation. "Okay," he said. "Five days."

Darcy stretched his arms above his head, his shirt rising to reveal a sliver of skin and the start of a trail of hair from his belly button which disappeared below the waistband of his pants. "I should get going." He smiled, then turned. "I'll show myself out." He raised his hand. "See you in the morning."

Five days.

Adrian slouched and leaned his head against the back of the sofa as he heard the soft click of the door shutting. Thoughts and emotions swirled together. Closing his eyes, he rested his hand over his erection. "Five days, really?" It appeared his body thought differently.

Darcy.

He spread his legs, opened his robe, then slipped his hand in the front of his briefs and took hold of his dick.

Darcy.

As he made slow, steady strokes along his length, Adrian pictured Darcy's face, his full, fuckable lips, his dark eyes, and his intensity. His imagination drew his gaze lower to what might lie beneath the tailored suits and fitted dress pants, to smooth skin and firm, defined muscle.

Adrian lifted his hips, fumbled to push down his underwear until his erection sprang free. He bit on his lip, muting the small sounds rising in his throat as he shifted his pace, and imagined Darcy's hand instead of his own, tugging and teasing him to the height of climax. Quicker, harder, his fist caught his balls on each desperate thrust.

Darcy.

He pictured Darcy above him, strong hands pushing his legs back, stretching him open, then filling his body. Possibilities ached through him like an echo from the future of what might be. From the pleasurable burn of Darcy entering him to the slap of sweat glistening skin on skin from every violently eager thrust.

Fuck.

"Darcy." Adrian opened his eyes as he lurched forward with a final rough stroke. His dick twitched as he came across his stomach in a heated mess. "Fuck." He slowly moved his hand over his easing erection, then let go. With a sigh, he stared at the ceiling.

It was going to be a long five days.

"GOOD MORNING." Abby beamed at Adrian as he joined her for breakfast. She wore a hooded sweatshirt and a long denim skirt, and she'd pulled her hair into a messy bun on the top of her head.

Had he missed the memo about it being Casual Tuesday?

Adrian pulled out the chair beside her. "What are you so happy about?"

"You mean what's not to be happy about?" She pushed a glass of orange juice in his direction, then picked up her own glass of what looked like grapefruit juice.

"I'm to presume your talk with Graham went well then?" He hadn't properly spoken to her beyond a series of texts after returning from the beach. He'd been too busy hiding in his room and not wanting to face Darcy.

She nodded. "All is well in Abbyland."

Adrian laughed. "Maybe I'll come visit Abbyland."

"Oh?" Abby narrowed her eyes. "My big sister senses are tingling. What's up?"

Crap. Abby had always been quick to figure out when something was on Adrian's mind be it family stuff, work stuff, or his car wreck of a love life.

"Nothing," he said. He hoped there was nothing in his voice that would draw her curiosity further. "I just like seeing you happy." He folded his arms and rested them against the edge of the table. He scanned the room before asking, "Where's Darcy?"

"Pretty sure he's filling his plate with bacon."

"Can't argue with that." Adrian raised an eyebrow as he eyed Abby's breakfast of fruit, muesli, and yogurt.

Abby picked up her spoon. "You eating?"

Adrian exhaled. "In a bit." He ran his finger along a crease in the tablecloth. He wasn't feeling all that hungry.

I could take a muffin for later.

"Morning."

Adrian glanced up to find Darcy standing in front of him. "Hi." He grinned as he stared at the pile of food on Darcy's plate. "Did you leave anything for anyone else?"

Darcy pulled a comical face, then put his plate in the place opposite Adrian, on the other side of Abby. "Breakfast is the most important meal of the day." He sat.

"Haven't there been studies that say otherwise?" Adrian looked at Abby.

"How should I know?" she said.

"Because science."

"Do I look like a nutritionist?"

Adrian stared at her messy hair. "You're right. You do look more 'mad scientist' this morning."

Abby raised her hands and shrugged.

Darcy chuckled and picked up his mug. The scent of coffee wafted across the table as he blew on the hot liquid. "Anyway, did you sleep well? Your foot giving you any bother?"

"Oh yeah, your foot," Abby said around a mouthful of breakfast. "That was a cunning plan, Ade."

"Cunning plan?"

Abby swallowed. "Got yourself an excuse to get out of last night's dinner and speeches." She stuck up her thumb. "Good for you, bro."

"Shut up." He sat back. "It actually hurt. There was blood and limping and everything. Tell her, Darcy."

Darcy looked up from his plate. "What?" He stabbed his fork into his pile of bacon, blueberry pancakes, and maple syrup. "What did I do?"

Abby snorted a laugh.

"Forget it. Go back to your bacon."

Darcy furrowed his brow but seemed to decide his breakfast was of greater importance than figuring out what was going on between Adrian and Abby. As he forced a slab of pancakes into his mouth, syrup dripped onto his lower lip.

Adrian fixated on the glistening droplet, the urge rising to reach across the table and wipe it away. Other scenarios came to his mind. Ones in which he ran his fingers over Darcy's lips, where he smeared the sweet syrup across Darcy's skin, where he would lick the spot clean, where he would kiss him. He lowered his gaze as Darcy flicked out his tongue.

It was just five days. Five long days until he could act on his feelings.

Five days.

Chapter Nine

OF COURSE, THE DAYS CRAWLED BY FOR DARCY. THERE WAS probably a law or something about how when he wanted something badly enough the clock slowed down. Five days had dwindled to three, but the urge to touch and taste Adrian was intense and all-consuming. By unspoken agreement, they'd stayed away from each other, or at least as far as they could at a family wedding.

They had the stag day to get through. A whole day dedicated to all things men, with stops for beer and too much toasting after an afternoon at a health spa.

The spa had been torturous, and he'd suggested to Abby that maybe they didn't need him to go, but she insisted it would be good for Adrian.

Good for Adrian maybe, but what about him?

The discomfort had started way before he got sight of Adrian in only a small white towel. No, it began when the groom had caught him in the sauna.

"How do you stay so fit? Is it an army thing?" Justin asked him, completely naked and staring down at his stomach, patting it gently. "I can't seem to keep up the exercise needed, apart from sex of course. Is that how you do it? Sex?"

What scared Darcy was that Justin actually thought this was a good thing to talk about.

"I never kiss and tell." He stood up to leave.

"I know Adrian is gay, so, like, loads of sex, right, but it's not like Abby seems like a person who wants sex, you know?"

"What?" Darcy rounded on the man, who took a step back, his bare ass hitting the wooden seat.

"I meant no disrespect," he began but didn't get a chance to finish that sentence.

"You see, Justin, that is exactly what you did do. You disrespected my girlfriend, her brother, and not only that, but you sound like an asshole."

Justin held up his hands. "Genuinely, I'm sorry. It's no big. If they were here, they would know I was only joking."

He'd left then before he had to listen to any more of Justin's crap, striding down the corridor and connecting head on with Adrian who was looking down at his phone.

"Sorry, I…" Adrian glanced up and blinked at him, and then his gaze went from Darcy's face and deliberately down his body. Darcy's fingers itched with the need to grab this man and shove him into the nearest room with a lock on the door.

Instead, he let his temper take control, anything to calm the hell down.

"Your cousin is an asshole."

"Okay?" Adrian began cautiously. "Tell me something I don't know."

There was the sound of a door closing behind them, and Adrian tugged Darcy back around the corner.

"What happened?"

Darcy shook his head. Talking was overrated, and he'd promised not to touch Adrian when all he wanted to do was do that very thing. He knew he couldn't stay in here, not with a half-dressed Adrian and his cousin who needed to be taken down a peg or two.

So he found the changing rooms, dressed, and left.

Anything to keep his sanity.

He didn't get far, Justin huffing and puffing up behind him, in a robe and slippers, in the middle of the parking lot.

"Wait, look, I didn't know how to talk to you okay, and I was nervous, and I was trying to be one of the boys as they might do in the army or something. I apologize completely."

There was honesty in the genuine apology, and what Darcy should do now was agree it was over, but he was antsy, so he crossed his arms over his chest and saw Justin wince. He held the stance for a few moments and then nodded.

"Apology accepted."

Justin reached out to pump Darcy's hand furiously before backing away and shuffling toward the center with a small wave.

IT SEEMED Darcy didn't have to be an expert to see the simmering tension in Charlotte. For someone who took pride in her clothes and the mask of makeup she wore, she seemed to be slipping. He saw her before Abby and Adrian did, a specter looming at the door, tears in her eyes. He left the breakfast table immediately, not entirely sure what he was doing, but knowing that this wasn't good. He was used to handling live munitions, and this situation looked as if it was going to blow up in everyone's face. He reached her as she stepped inside, gently encouraging her back out and into the hallway.

"I'm sorry," she said. "I didn't mean to kiss you." She shook off his gentle hold.

"It's all good."

She peered around him, "I want to talk to Abby."

He moved to block her without making it too obvious. "How about we get coffee and chill for a while?" Before she could voice her disagreement, he steered her to the private lounge and chose a corner booth.

"I should get Graham." He moved to leave.

"No, he doesn't. I didn't…" She started crying again.

With an internal sigh, he sat down and passed her his napkin, even though she had a perfectly good one for herself.

"Who should I get for you then? Your mom?" He knew that Charlotte's mom was part of the coven as he had been introduced.

"God, no," she said with horror in her voice. "I just need to sit here."

"Okay," he murmured, but that didn't seem like a very good plan at all.

"Abby is gorgeous," she said after a short time.

"She is."

"And exceptionally brilliant in what she does."

He nodded then, wondering where this was leading.

"It's no wonder my husband would rather have her than me." She looked right at him. "You know that, right? You're just a stopgap, a temporary thing until she takes Graham from me." Her hands slipped from the table and rested in her lap. "You can go."

His particular code of chivalry meant he wasn't going anywhere, and he called over for coffee and sat back for the long haul. In all that time, she said nothing but folded and unfolded the napkin he'd given her, creasing it and turning it, and evidently thinking things through.

After ten or so minutes, she stood, inclined her head to him, and left.

That was one of the weirdest things he'd ever been part of, and he needed some Abby/Adrian normality quick.

They were still at breakfast, Abby on her iPad, Adrian sipping coffee and staring out at the ocean. He slid back into his seat.

Adrian smiled at him, raising a single eyebrow in question, but Darcy shook his head subtly, and that was the end of it.

Somehow, he made it through the day, was social when he needed to be, sat quietly when Abby was working, and refused the offer to go for a walk with Adrian. That would have been too dangerous. As it was, it was hard to check out Adrian and not imagine all the kinds of things he could do with him when he had him naked under him in bed.

Dinner tonight was the last event before tomorrow's wedding, an elaborate affair that involved more speeches. How much more did anyone have to say he didn't understand, but he listened dutifully and played the part of Abby's boyfriend perfectly. So well that he kept getting approving glances from her mom and the other members of the coven.

"I need to run some statistical analysis," Abby whispered to him, and he turned into her as if he was listening to her whisper sweet nothings in his ear.

"Of course," he said, and when they'd made their excuses, he walked up to their room with her and tried not to think about the look that Adrian had given him when they'd left.

One more day.

He went for a walk to clear his head, to lose himself in the sound of the ocean and the cool breeze. This job wasn't all bad. It wasn't exactly what he'd planned for his life. He'd wanted to be a career soldier, expected it really, but he got to stay in places like this, and that was a bonus. There was rain in the air tonight, and he headed back to the house by way of the park area that ran from the house, through trees and bushes and down to the cliffs. He was entirely alone and lost himself in thoughts of what he could do to Adrian once they passed this no-touching freeze.

He hadn't felt like this in a long time, with lust coursing through his body and making him irrational, but there was something about Adrian that made him want to get right inside his head. Maybe on the first date, they could just fuck and get it out of their system or possibly just sit somewhere and kiss. He'd gotten himself off to thoughts of Adrian too many times to count now, and the images he had conjured up in his head of the gorgeous man were detailed.

The sound of voices had him turning to avoid them, and then he picked up on who it was talking. Graham and Charlotte, discussing something heatedly. He so didn't want to get in the middle of another domestic, but there had been sadness in Charlotte's eyes, and he had immediately considered that it was Graham who had put it there. Was she trapped in this marriage? Was Graham the bad guy in this?

"… being irrational, sweetheart." Graham's voice was uneven. He sounded almost desperate.

"That's your go-to, isn't it? The sentence you always use when I cry. Why is it you think I can't have rational reasons for crying? I'm tired, and I feel sick, and I want to cry."

"So, tell me, what did I do? What went wrong?"

"We're going around in circles."

"No, we're not. You know I love you. I asked you to marry me, didn't I?"

"You think that proves anything?"

"Oh my god, Charlotte, I can't win. I love you so much that it hurts, and this thing with Abby is work, nothing more."

"I want to believe you—"

Her words stopped suddenly, and Darcy took a step closer and then realized when he heard her low moan and heated words that he'd be walking in on the two of them making up. He backed away slowly.

"I'm sorry," he heard Graham say.

"I love you," Charlotte said back.

He hurried away, back to the hotel, made it to the elevator, and was all the way in when the couple he'd just eavesdropped on ran into it, wet from the rain and laughing.

"Hi," he said, in case they hadn't spotted him in the corner of the elevator.

Charlotte smiled at him, and she truly was beautiful when she smiled, her ordinarily perfect hair tousled from wind and kissing, and her eyes sparkling. Loving Graham and knowing she was loved back made her light up from inside.

The knock on his door after he got back made him smile, thinking it was Adrian on the other side. But it wasn't. It was Charlotte looking drier and in jeans and a T-shirt.

"Is Abby here?"

"I'm here," Abby said from behind him.

"Can I come in, just for a moment?" Charlotte asked.

"Not really," Abby snapped.

"I get that, but I want to say I am sorry about what I sent you in those texts. It was vile, and I was just trying to get you to stay away from the wedding. But you came anyway. It didn't matter what I said, and you are a braver woman than me." She moved back to the door. "Anyway, Graham says I need to be better, not such a bitch, and I can't promise I'll change overnight. We're not all as settled in life as you are."

Darcy wanted to interject then, call Charlotte out for that

statement which made it sound as if it was somehow Abby's fault that she had her work and her life in a good place.

"Shit, I said that wrong." She scrubbed her eyes. Then she held out a hand to Abby. "Truce? Will you accept? I'm sorry."

Abby simply shook Charlotte's hand, and that was it. Done.

When Charlotte had left, he turned to a bemused Abby.

"You're a better person than I am," he said.

Abby huffed, then grinned. "Believe me. It took a lot not to smack her with the nearest soft object."

"Soft?"

"Wouldn't want to hurt her now, would I?"

THE SUN SHONE on the day of the wedding. A beautiful summer's day after last night's gentle rain had freshened everything, and everyone appeared to be in high spirits. Darcy had spotted Charlotte and Graham holding hands at breakfast and smiling at each other like idiots. To his knowledge, Abby had been on the phone with Michael three times this morning so far, and now waiting for the ceremony, he was sitting next to Adrian, and he wanted some of that flirting that everyone else had going on.

"You like Thai food?" he asked Adrian.

"Always."

Darcy lowered his voice. "You like it as takeout?"

"Even more."

Darcy took out his phone and typed out his address, handing the phone to Adrian and waiting for him to type in the number. Now he had Adrian's number, and Adrian had his address.

Then there was only one more thing to say.

"As soon as you can, right?"

Adrian dipped his eyes and then looked up at him. "As soon as I can."

The ceremony wasn't too long, and when the guests all spilled out onto the extensive lawns, it was time for the final part of his pretense. He took Abby by the hand and tugged her away from the leading group, far enough so no one could hear, close enough that they could see.

"So this is it," he murmured. "You sure this is how you want it to go?"

She placed a hand on his chest. "Can you imagine the plans the coven could already be making for my wedding? I can't bear that, and they need to know it's over with you."

"Am I looking suitably regretful?" he asked and placed a hand over hers.

"You could try a little more, maybe?" she said thoughtfully but with a smirk on her lips. "What about me? Am I looking like I've made a tough decision?"

"The hardest," he said. "Say something else."

"I may have told Michael that I met a man at the wedding and then sent him a photo," she admitted, and the smile grew a little too much for it to look like she was genuinely breaking up with him.

"Drop the smile." He leaned closer. "And?"

"We sexted." She was biting her lip to stop the grin. "And we're *so* getting it on when I get back, test tubes and Bunsen burners falling off the counters."

"I like you a lot," Darcy said. "It's been fun."

She leaned against him then, her face away from family. "I so know you want to bone my brother," she said, and he had to try really hard not to snort with laughter.

"Maybe so."

"I know he'd be up for it, so to speak."

Darcy thought about the kiss and the tension that had built between them over the last couple of days. A look here, a touch there, and so much unspoken between them.

"I think he would be," Darcy admitted.

"So, we'll see each other. Soon."

"Soon."

She sighed then. "Thank you for this, Darcy. I know you're all paid for, but you went above and beyond."

"You're welcome." He pressed a kiss to her hair. "Are you ready to handle the fallout?"

"Photos are next. That will keep everyone busy."

"Okay then. Ready?"

They separated, and he bent over her hand, kissing the back of it, and gave her a final nod. Then without a backward glance, he went into the hotel, past the family, past Adrian, who watched him go.

He was packed and into his car within fifteen minutes and on the highway soon after. The drive was only four hours, broken up by stopping for coffee in Newhaven, and then he was home, leaving his car in the underground parking and going up to his apartment. New York looked fine today from his window, a sliver of the Hudson River in the far distance, the skyscrapers of Manhattan laid out in front of him.

He drank coffee, unpacked, showered, and waited for Adrian.

Chapter Ten

"WHAT ARE YOU DOING?" ADRIAN PUSHED DOWN THE handle on his suitcase. He stared at Abby, who was kneeling on one of the sofas in reception with her arms draped over the furniture's back.

"Moping," Abby said and gave a weighty sigh. She curled down her bottom lip and leaned her head to one side.

Adrian rolled his eyes. "Poor thing." He was tired and irritable. He hadn't slept well. It seemed his brain had decided to say "screw you" to slumber and had instead opted for hours of playing out what might happen when he was reunited with Darcy. Everything from marriage and kids to a slammed door in his face.

"I've just broken up with my boyfriend. Let me wallow." She raised her head and said somewhat dramatically, "Will I ever love again?"

Darcy had made a quick exit after the wedding. Though he had been contracted until the Saturday, it seemed he and Abby had talked it through and decided straight after the wedding ceremony would be a better time. That way, Darcy could avoid appearing in too many of the official photographs.

"Maybe you could *text* Michael to ease your pain."

A few glasses of wine at last night's reception, and Abby had gushed nonstop about her lab buddy. It seemed things were actually moving forward for them, both in terms of their research and their relationship toward something beyond just colleagues. It was nice to see her enthusiastic about something other than work.

Abby did her best to suppress the rising smile on her lips. "Maybe." She rested her head in her hands. "What about you?"

Adrian checked his phone. "What about me?"

"Any plans for after you leave?"

A mutual *breakup* had always been the intended conclusion to Abby and Darcy's contract, with the excuse that the week together had made them realize they were better suited to being friends than lovers or something along those lines. But with the end to their pretend relationship, Abby was now in need of a ride home. "I don't know. Unpack, do laundry, restock the fridge." He'd be glad to get out of there and home, back to his modest life in the suburbs.

Abby pursed her lips. "So you're not going to go see a certain someone?"

"I don't know." Adrian stared at his feet.

"The guy just got dumped. He might appreciate the company."

Adrian sighed. He wasn't sure what was for the best. It wasn't that he didn't want to see Darcy, just the memory of the man saying "fuck" had kept him from going completely insane the last five days, but was it really okay? "You'd be all right with that?"

"Why wouldn't I be?" She tilted her head. "I might have

my nose stuck in data half the time, but I'm not completely oblivious." She checked around for who might have been within earshot before saying, "You like him, and I got the feeling he likes you too."

"You didn't pay out all that money so I'd end up with a date."

"I didn't. I paid for Darcy to be *my* date. He did his job, kept up appearances to the end, and now it's over. What happens after has nothing to do with me. However..." She met his eyes.

"What?"

"If things go places, you're explaining it to Mom." She leaned back. "And in no part of that explanation will you bring up anything concerning my and Darcy's little business arrangement."

Adrian parted his lips. Where would he even begin to explain what had happened? He shook his head. "I think we're getting ahead of ourselves. We might... He might not want anything serious."

Abby dragged her hand down the length of her ponytail. She turned to sit properly on the sofa, then looked over her shoulder and said, "I guess you should go find out."

SHOULD I BE HERE?

Adrian stood outside Darcy's apartment and eyed the number on the door. He could only get away with delaying the inevitable for a short while as Darcy had already buzzed him into the building. He raised his hand.

What do I even want to happen?

"Grow a pair, Adrian." He knocked and was surprised when Darcy opened it almost instantly. Had he been waiting on the other side?

"Hey." Darcy smiled brightly and outstretched his arm to welcome Adrian inside.

"Hi." Adrian stepped into the apartment. "Sorry for the short notice. I wasn't sure whether I'd head home after dropping Abby at hers." He clasped his hands together. "I know you said as soon as I could, but I didn't want to impose on you so soon after having already spent the week with us."

Darcy shook his head. "You're not imposing."

Adrian worried his lip and tried to relax by checking out Darcy's apartment. The front entrance opened onto one large room. The living/dining area was separated from the kitchen by a breakfast bar. The apartment was furnished modestly, clean lines, and no clutter. It suited the clean-cut, all-business Darcy Adrian had grown accustomed to. Smart, well dressed, straightforward.

"You're sure?" *Why am I still questioning it?* He turned around when Darcy shut the door. He swallowed hard as he met Darcy's dark gaze.

Darcy didn't say anything, simply closed the gap, and before Adrian could utter in confusion, Darcy was in front of him, his hands on Adrian's shoulders as he pulled him toward him. He then tucked one of his fingers under Adrian's chin, tilting back Adrian's head.

"I… We…" At that point, Adrian's brain decided to short circuit.

God, he smells good.

The familiar scent of Darcy's cologne hit the back of his throat as he looked up into his eyes.

Though there couldn't have been more than a couple of inches difference in their height, in that instant Darcy seemed so much bigger, had such a presence that Adrian longed to be enveloped by Darcy's strong embrace and his own strong feelings of desire for him.

Any opportunity to articulate those emotions was lost when Darcy pressed his mouth to Adrian's in a firm kiss. His lips were cooler than Adrian had imagined, but no less welcoming as Adrian felt the last embers of doubt fizzle from his body.

Darcy pulled back and held Adrian's face. "Does that answer your question?" His palms were warm, and he gently pushed back Adrian's hair, curling his fingers behind Adrian's ear.

"Remind me, what was the question?"

Darcy chuckled and patted his cheek. "Drink?"

"Sure."

"Wine? A beer? Soda?"

Adrian followed Darcy as he headed for the refrigerator. "I'm driving, so soda's fine."

"Sprite okay?"

"Sure. Thank you."

"No problem." Darcy stopped and turned around. "I meant to ask for your jacket."

Adrian glanced down. "Oh, right."

"You were planning on staying, right?" Darcy raised his eyebrows, creasing his forehead as he met Adrian's eyes. "Want that Thai food we talked about?"

I want that. Adrian shrugged off his jacket. "Food sounds great." He held it out to Darcy, who rounded the kitchen island to take it from him.

"I'll put it on the bed."

"Uh-huh." Adrian blinked. *Bed?* He pushed his hands into his back pockets and watched Darcy cross the room. "How was your drive home yesterday?" He caught his lower lip between his teeth as Darcy entered the bedroom. The end of the bed was visible, the base low and upholstered in dark brown leather. The dresser Adrian could make out was wooden, sturdy, and stained dark, and a tone-matching piece of artwork hung on the wall.

"Yeah, was a straightforward run, thankfully." Darcy pulled the door closed behind him and returned to the kitchen.

Adrian took a few steps and gazed around the room. His eyes settled on a photograph on a sideboard behind the couch. He tilted his head as he studied the image, which was of a group of men, soldiers, arms thrown over each other's shoulders, smiles on their faces. It took him a moment to spot Darcy, who was clearly younger when the photograph had been taken. His hair was more closely shorn, his beard simply stubble, but it was definitely him. The same smile. The same dark but warm, gaze.

I wonder where he was. The image had a yellowish-orange tint to it, probably reflecting the surroundings. *Overseas, somewhere.* Adrian wasn't sure he should pry into Darcy's Army past.

"You?" Darcy placed two glasses filled with Sprite on the counter.

"It was okay. Tiring."

"I get you."

Adrian laughed. "I meant Abby. She seemed to have energy to spare and wouldn't shut up."

Darcy parted his lips. "Ah." He pushed one of the glasses toward Adrian.

Adrian stared at the bubbles rising in the glass. "Look I just…" He sighed. "I wanted to say thank you."

"For what?"

"For the week. For having Abby's back. For being professional." Adrian ran his thumb over his stud earring. "For not letting me screw it all up." He realized Darcy had moved to his side of the island.

"How would you have screwed it up?"

He pulled on his ear. "I kissed you. I shouldn't have." He blinked as Darcy wrapped his hand around his wrist and slowly pulled down his arm.

"That habit of yours, with your ear. It's kind of cute, you know?"

Heat rose in Adrian's cheeks.

"Anyway, I think you'll find I kissed you first, so if anyone was going to get the blame for messing up, it would be me." He was still holding Adrian by the wrist. "It was a mistake, but we know that it wasn't a *mistake*."

Adrian raised his eyes.

"In that moment, kissing you was all I could think about. In fact, I don't think I've ever wanted to do anything as much as I did right then."

His voice.

"Except maybe now." Darcy tugged on Adrian's arm, pulling him close.

His kiss.

Darcy pressed their mouths together for the second time in the space of minutes, and Adrian was okay with that. He was in a strange and unfamiliar place, and yet, Adrian, for some reason, already felt as if he was home. Darcy was warm, his hold comforting, and his kiss made Adrian feel wanted.

He's so warm.

Darcy breathed in deeply and hugged Adrian.

Adrian swallowed back the tumbling feeling and closed his eyes as Darcy's thigh brushed his crotch. His imagination took over, flashes of skin on skin. He wanted Darcy, but he couldn't bring himself to tell Darcy that. He was scared. Scared that he liked Darcy in a way that, if all Darcy wanted was a one-time thing, it might break his heart.

"I can wait."

The sound of Darcy's voice reverberated through him. Had he said his thoughts out loud?

Darcy relaxed his hold. "Let's eat. Let's talk." He pressed a kiss to Adrian's cheek, then took a step back. "Let's spend some time together."

Adrian nodded. He could do that.

With a smile, Darcy opened a drawer and pulled out a menu. "So, first things first. Food." He listed off a variety of dishes, some Adrian had never heard of. "So what do you think?"

Adrian eyed the menu. He hated to dampen Darcy's apparent passion for food, but he had no strong feelings about what to eat. "I'm happy with whatever."

"Really?" Darcy quirked an eyebrow.

"Honestly. I'm the kind of person who just orders the same thing every single time, so it'll be nice to try something new." He smiled. "I'll consider it an adventure."

"Living dangerously again?"

Adrian lowered his head. Those had been his words of encouragement to get Darcy to spend time with him on the day they had ended down at the beach. "Sometimes taking a risk pays off." He lifted his gaze to meet Darcy's.

"It does?"

Adrian smiled. "In my experience, yes." He stepped forward and pressed his hand to Darcy's chest. "And hopefully, this will too."

With a nod, Darcy pulled out his cell phone. "I hope so, too."

Chapter Eleven

THE FOOD DIDN'T TAKE LONG TO BE DELIVERED, BUT NOT much of it got eaten, not when Adrian kept licking his fingers free of sweet chili sauce and making obscene sounds of pleasure that went straight to Darcy's cock.

There was so much enjoyment in Adrian. The way he tried every single new dish and articulated his thoughts, sometimes with words, but mostly with groans and moans, and the diving in for more.

Darcy had long since given up on eating just watched Adrian with his unabashed enjoyment of the new experiences. He wanted to kiss him so badly that eating had fallen to second place on the list. They'd waited a long time to kiss properly, and they were in Darcy's place. No one could see them, so why were they eating? Why weren't they kissing?

Adrian tilted his head back to get a long noodle into his mouth all in one go, then wiped his sticky fingers with a wet wipe. He used a fork to eat a mouthful of Shrimp Pad Thai, sucking at the sauce and sighing, and that was it. Game over.

Calmly, gently, Darcy took the food and the fork he was using away from Adrian then slid back on the sofa, taking

Adrian with him. With a pliant man willing to be positioned just so, he finally had Adrian straddling his lap, and he didn't give him time to complain about the lack of food or the manhandling. He went straight for a kiss, cradling Adrian's head and pulling him close, tilting his face so their lips could slot into place with ease.

The taste of him was everything that Darcy had remembered, and all he wanted right now. Adrian was breaking away from him, just a little, separating the kiss, asking about more or food or something Darcy couldn't make out.

"Stop talking," Darcy ordered.

Adrian huffed a laugh but didn't argue, wriggling to sit closer and wrapping his hands around Darcy's neck. The time for talking was well and truly over.

The kiss deepened, Darcy holding him still, his grip tight and sure, and Adrian groaned low in his throat, scrabbling to hold Darcy and finally twisting his hands in his hair.

Darcy encouraged Adrian forward as he shuffled lower down the cushions, and at that point, he couldn't have moved, even if he wanted. Adrian was so pliant, and Darcy wanted to take this anywhere that wasn't the damn sofa. Only, he didn't want to move from there, not until he had Adrian gasping and begging and so close that one touch would send him over the edge. He lifted Adrian's shirt, yanking at the fabric and popping buttons in a desperate need to touch his skin.

"Sit back," he ordered, and Adrian complied, balancing himself while keeping his fingers laced in Darcy's hair. He tugged at the remaining stubborn button, and then he had his hands on Adrian's skin, and it was everything he remembered. Soft and warm, and god, when he ran his fingers over Adrian's nipples, the way he gasped and arched into the touch was the best thing in the entire world.

It seemed his nipples were hardwired to his cock, and Darcy spent a long time caressing them gently, then teasing them, twisting until Adrian's breathing was out of kilter.

Taking pity on him, he stopped, and Adrian gripped his hair tighter.

"Let go," Darcy commanded.

Adrian's eyes opened, his gaze fixed on Darcy. He didn't seem to understand, and then abruptly he did, releasing his fingers from their grip and pulling his hands away. He immediately slipped to the right and gasped in shock until Darcy held his hips.

"I've got you," he said, and immediately Adrian relaxed, his lips parting and the tension easing.

The only thing holding Adrian upright was Darcy, and it was Darcy who held all the cards. Just as he liked it.

"Open your pants."

Adrian nodded and then undid the top button, pushed down the zipper, and Darcy felt for himself that this sexy man had nothing on underneath. He groaned as he circled his hand around Adrian's prick and reveled in the fact that Adrian had stopped writhing on his lap and instead had gone deadly still.

"I've waited too long for this," Darcy murmured, slipping his fingers as far as could and then back, twisting at the top and watching as Adrian closed his eyes. He wanted them open, so he could watch them darken with passion and desire, but that could be next time. Right now, he wanted Adrian coming over his hand.

But not too fast; he slowed his movements, watching the tension in every line of Adrian's lithe form, the sweat that dampened his skin, the noises he was making.

"Please…"

Darcy could finish this here and now. A couple more twists, a tug on Adrian's nipples, and he could leave him wrecked. But, when Adrian opened his eyes and looked right at him, let out that plea, he knew he had to get this into the bedroom. He bunched his muscles, scooted them to the edge, kissed away Adrian's disappointment, then tugged him to the bedroom.

"You want to do this?" Darcy asked, giving Adrian plenty of time to cool down, needing to know that he really wanted this.

Adrian shoved at him, stalked to the bed, and flung open the top drawer of the bedside cabinet, rummaging and pulling out lube and condoms with a triumphant shout. Then he fell back onto the mattress, arms and legs spread.

"Come on, then."

Darcy fell for him right there in that moment. The way Adrian smiled, the need in him, the desperate heat that had built between them. This man was fire, and Darcy accepted he was going to get burned.

He didn't waste any time stripping Adrian until his lover was gloriously naked in the center of Darcy's huge bed. He made quick work of undressing himself and crawled onto the bed to cage Adrian in his arms.

"Last chance," Darcy warned with a smile.

Adrian shook his head and tangled his fingers in Darcy's hair, pulling him down for a kiss and sighing as Darcy's weight blanketed him.

"I love this," he murmured, wriggling until he was in just the right position, his cock right alongside Darcy's, pushing between it and the crease of a thigh and then arching up into him.

If Darcy wasn't careful, he was going to lose all control, and he had to slow this down. He'd never had a lover who was so on his wavelength, whose body responded to his touches in all the right ways. He eased away a little and pressed one hand to Adrian's thigh, stopping him from moving. Adrian stilled in an instant, blinking up at Darcy and then releasing his hold in Darcy's hair. Unbidden, he put his hands to the headboard and kept them there, and then his tongue darted out to wet his lips. Darcy couldn't take his eyes off the hands on the headboard.

He's going to kill me with all this sexy shit.

"Maybe next time you could tie me so I stay still," Adrian murmured and tilted his head.

Darcy put on a condom, took the lube and pressed his fingers to Adrian's ass, his other hand moving from thigh to cock, enclosing Adrian in his fist and moving his hand only a little. This way, he was pinned again and writhing on Darcy's finger as he pressed inside.

"You want me to get one of my ties and wrap it around your wrists, huh?" He crooked his finger, added the tip of a second, and waited, looking for discomfort or any sign that Adrian needed to get off the bed. When there was nothing, he kept talking, adding more lube and then wiping some on his own cock. "Maybe get you to the edge and leave you there, come back time and time again…"

Adrian closed his eyes briefly and then tilted his hips as Darcy slid his knees under Adrian's thighs.

"Talk to me, Adrian," Darcy murmured. He eased into Adrian's ass, the tip, nothing more, and waited, "Tell me."

"More," Adrian gasped. "all of it."

Slowly, he rocked inside, all the time kissing, playing with Adrian's cock, working him up to the edge again.

"I'm…" was all Adrian could manage.

Darcy could tell he was close. He angled himself as best he could. The tightness excited him beyond anything he had imagined. Then he twisted his fingers around Adrian's cock, and it was done. Over.

Adrian went absolutely silent again, exposing his neck for kisses, and Darcy sucked him there, murmured praises against Adrian's skin as wet heat collected over his hand. Then it was his turn, one press, another, and the orgasm was intense, stealing his thoughts and actions and leaving him breathless. He called Adrian's name, and then when the very last rush of lust passed, he collapsed boneless, making sure not to squash Adrian, and only when he was done did he roll to one side, dealing with the condom and trying to catch his breath.

Adrian's breathing was ragged, and he was laughing again as if sex between them was the happiest thing in his world.

"We need to do that again," he whispered against Darcy's neck. "Right now."

And all Darcy could do was hold him tight, awkward and messy and sated, and pray his recovery time was quick.

Because he sure as hell wanted more of Adrian as soon as he was able to.

Chapter Twelve

ADRIAN FLINCHED AWAKE. HIS CHEEK TWITCHED AS HE slowly opened his eyes. What had woken him? He was sure he'd heard a dull knock. Was someone at the door? Or just part of a dream? He let out a sigh, flicked out his tongue to moisten his lips, and watched the sway of drapes as a breeze blew in through an open window.

Wait. Adrian lifted his head. That wasn't his window. Those weren't his drapes. *This isn't my bed.*

"Phone," he uttered and pushed himself up on one arm. He rubbed his eye and dragged his phone to the edge of the nightstand. Pressing the button, he checked the time. "Crap." It was nearly noon.

He sighed again, dropping back against the pillow. Last night had been something of a whirlwind, and he had allowed himself to be swept up in Darcy and his desires.

Darcy.

Adrian turned his head. Darcy wasn't there. Idly, he drew his hand over the crumpled sheets on Darcy's side of the bed. They were cool to the touch.

How long had he been gone?

Closing his eyes, Adrian rested his arm across his face. As enjoyable as last night had been, he couldn't ignore the grip of doubt on his heart. Too many men had already caused cracks in the fragile organ, betrayed him, and trampled his feelings to dust. He wanted something from Darcy, and he hoped to hell Darcy would be able to give it to him.

All that talk of being tied down? It wasn't playing. And Darcy was all toppy and growly, and Adrian wanted that so much.

"So what now?" he mumbled against his skin, waiting to be told to leave. The hairs on his forearm brushed his lips.

"How about lunch?"

Adrian lowered his arm and was surprised to find Darcy standing beside the bed. "When did you…?"

"What can I say? Stealthy is my middle name." Darcy sat on the bed, pulling up a knee as he leaned forward and planted a kiss on Adrian's mouth. "Actually, it's not. It's Jonathan."

"Okay." Adrian chuckled and rubbed his hand over his face. "You should have woken me."

"Why?" Darcy tilted his head.

"Because."

Darcy shrugged. "You looked cute, so I didn't want to disturb you. Plus, I imagine it's been a tiring few days for you, hanging out with family."

Adrian couldn't deny his family exhausted him. "It is Sunday, isn't it?"

Darcy laughed. "It is."

"Thank God." He leaned his head slightly. "Have you got the day off? No new jobs?" Adrian was tired, but even he realized his tone sounded off.

Darcy was thoughtful as he stared at the window.

Silence enveloped the room, and Adrian didn't know

what to say to lift the strange mood that had fallen between them. He knew what was happening here, Darcy was recalling that he had a job to do, and that Adrian had just been a loosely connected part of his last job. No sense in thinking this was anything more now they'd actually slept together. But then, Adrian didn't want Darcy doing any more jobs where he got to fuck the brother of the woman he was pretending to date. He didn't want to have to think that Darcy did this every time.

You know him better than that.

Adrian couldn't listen to his inner voice. He actually didn't know Darcy better than that at all. They'd spent the week trying to keep their hands off each other, and now they'd had their hands on each other. So what now? What was left?

It was Darcy who made the first move. Clearing his throat, he stood. "Come on. You can't stay in bed all day." He patted Adrian on the thigh. "Feel free to grab a shower. I hung a fresh towel behind the door. Plus, you can use anything you need in the bathroom, you know, toiletries or whatever." He paused for a moment, then added, "I'll be in the kitchen when you're ready." He flashed a bright smile, then left, pulling the door shut behind him.

Adrian's gaze lingered on the closed door. Had Darcy's smile been forced? Had Adrian pissed him off?

Lying here won't get me any answers.

Throwing back the sheet, he then rolled his legs over the side. Adrian clasped his hands together above his head and straightened his back.

To shower or not to shower?

He walked to the adjoining bathroom and stopped when he reached the basin. Above the bowl was a mirror, and Adrian studied himself. His hair stuck up in various directions, and his cheek was red and patterned with the imprint of Darcy's bedding.

Wonderful. Maybe if he asked nicely, Darcy would find a way to scrub the image from his memory.

Adrian turned around and eyed the towel. For some reason, he felt insecure about showering in another person's home. He glanced down. He was naked. It wasn't as if taking a shower was going to leave him in any more of a vulnerable state. "Whatever," he mumbled. He'd shower properly when he got home, so instead, he opted to quickly wash his face and flatten down his hair with water.

Roughly, he dried his hair. When he was done, he hung the towel over the side of the tub, then inspected the shelf of toiletries. It would be easy enough to head out to his car and collect some of his own things, but curiosity got the better of him. He eyed the various items before picking up the deodorant. He didn't use it straight away, instead spraying it in the air in front of him.

Darcy. He recalled the intoxicating sensation of Darcy holding him tightly, the feel of Darcy's skin against his. The scent was the same and yet subtly different. It was missing something.

After using the deodorant, he returned to the bedroom and dressed. Darcy was waiting for him when he emerged from the room.

"Everything okay?" Darcy asked. He was standing on the kitchen side of the island.

"Yes. Thanks." Adrian joined him at the counter, sliding onto one of the stools on the opposite side. "Did you go out this morning?" He rested his head in his hand and leaned on the counter.

"I did." Darcy drew a bread knife from the block. "The refrigerator was a little bare, so I went out to grab a few things." A shopping sat on the counter behind him. He smiled, turned around, and grabbed the bag. Placing it in front of Adrian, he then rolled down the top of the bag and pulled out a plastic tub and a baguette. "Not quite as good as your grandmother would have made it but…"

Adrian glanced from the bread to the label on the tub, realizing it was tomato soup. "You got that for me?" He didn't know what else to say, taken aback by Darcy's thoughtfulness.

"I hope you don't mind. I mean, I wasn't sure if I should because, well, you know, but I just saw it, and it made me smile when I remembered us talking back at the beach."

Adrian lowered his gaze.

"I didn't want to upset you or bring back sad memories." Darcy paused. "We can have something else—"

"No," Adrian said quickly. "No. It's fine. It's sweet you remembered. I didn't expect…" He pressed his hand over his heart. The warmth of what he could only describe as happiness spread beneath his palm. When he raised his head, Darcy was looking at him. As always, it was as if his dark eyes saw straight through Adrian.

"Say, do you have to head off soon, or do you have some time?" Darcy laid the knife on the counter.

Adrian shrugged. "I have some time. Why?"

"Spend the day with me. The afternoon."

Adrian pursed his lips. "And do what?" He spoke slowly, his words maybe more guarded than they should have been. As lovely as an afternoon in bed sounded, he wasn't sure it was what he wanted. Not right then. Though if that was all Darcy was interested in, Adrian was probably best figuring that out sooner than later or when he'd completely fallen for the man.

"Go out. Shopping, the park, um… I don't know. What do other people do on dates?"

Adrian didn't think he'd heard right.

"You want to go on a date?"

"Sure. Why not?"

There was a twinge, a tingly sensation in Adrian's chest. *Why are you acting so unsure all of a sudden? Stop being an idiot and say yes.* "Yes."

Darcy laughed. Then his expression became serious. "I want to say something. Will you hear me out?"

Adrian nodded.

"Cards on the table. Full disclosure. I love my job. I've met a lot of people, played boyfriend to both men and women, and I plan to keep doing that for the foreseeable future, but I don't plan to fall for any cute siblings." Darcy held Adrian's gaze. "So, if my job bothers you, I guess we say we had a great time and you head home. No harm done."

If it bothers me? Adrian had been messed about by men more times than he cared to remember. He figured it came down to whether or not he trusted Darcy. Or rather was he ready to trust him? He looked at Darcy, studied his expression.

I want to.

Adrian smiled. "I don't have to head home just yet." He took a slow breath. "If you're okay with that?"

Darcy grinned and leaned forward across the counter. He hooked his finger in the neck of Adrian's T-shirt and pulled him forward into a kiss. "I'm okay with that."

"WHERE ARE YOU?" Abby asked the instant Adrian answered his phone.

"Darcy's." *As I have been every spare moment since we*

came back from the wedding. It had been four weeks since that first sleepover, and to be honest, he really should've brought over more clothes. He couldn't keep borrowing Darcy's New York Rangers T-shirt to walk around the apartment in. Even though it did smell of Darcy, and even though it apparently got Darcy hot every single time he did wear it.

The sex had been off the charts, with and without the use of Darcy's incredible range of ties, and just the thought of seeing him made every moment they were apart full of expectation.

He'd been away the last few days on a job, acting as the boyfriend of a gay actor. Adrian wasn't sure what was worse. That it wasn't a woman, or that it was a man who would very definitely want to get into Darcy's pants. Who wouldn't want into his pants?

Apparently the actor was boring and arrogant and smelled of garlic. Was that true? Adrian wasn't sure, but Darcy's lovemaking didn't change, and he smiled and hugged Adrian at every possible chance.

"Hello? Adrian, you still there?"

"Sorry, I drifted." He changed the subject before she could ask questions he knew he didn't have the answers to. "So you know where I am. Where are you?"

"Michael's." She laughed, and there was the clink of what sounded like plates and cutlery. "We just finished lunch."

Adrian sat on the couch and smiled at Darcy as he passed him on his way to the bedroom. "That's great, Sis. Is that what you called to tell me?"

Abby made a strange huffed sound. "No, this is… I guess Mom didn't call you yet?"

"Mom? What about?" Adrian's stomach fell. His Mom had been quiet since the wedding, and a phone call from her normally meant some social occasion he needed to attend.

"Dad's sixtieth birthday is next month. Remember?"

Adrian sighed.

"You'd totally forgotten," Abby teased.

"I hadn't. I was choosing not to think about it."

"In the hope it would just go away?"

As per the Fitzgerald way, a sixtieth birthday meant a party, a big one, with people he didn't care to spend time with.

"Something like that." Adrian pulled down the zipper on his jacket. He and Darcy had barely stepped foot into the apartment when Abby had phoned. "So what exactly did Mom want?"

"To tell me that she expects both you and me to bring our boyfriends to the party."

Tensing his jaw, Adrian leaned his head to get a better view of Darcy through the open bedroom door. He was hanging up the new shirts he had bought on their shopping trip down Fifth Avenue.

"Boyfriend, huh?"

Darcy shot him a look. Despite hanging out and basically being in each other's pockets for a while, neither had brought up the B-word. He could almost see the question Darcy would ask. *Boyfriends? Is that what we are now?*

That was a discussion to have with wine and maybe after hot sex. Meanwhile, there was a more pressing issue to address. "Wait. What did Mom say when you told her about you and Darcy breaking up?"

Abby didn't reply, which was an answer in itself.

"Jeez. Abby. You haven't told her, have you? She still thinks you were really dating, doesn't she?"

"Well, here's the thing…"

"Abby."

"I've been busy with work, or rather I didn't want to have to explain it to her."

"What the hell, Abby. You think I do? She already stares at me as if I was permanently in the wrong on everything."

Abby sighed. "You'll be fine. You're way better at handling Mom than me. Besides you're clearly her favorite."

I was having a lovely day. We went shopping, grabbed coffee, ate hot dogs in the park. Just lovely. And now look at it.

"You know that's garbage," Adrian said.

"I really need to go. I should let you enjoy your afternoon."

"Really? You're dropping that bomb and hanging up."

"Love you."

Adrian was about to say more, but Abby had ended the call. "Love you, too," he mumbled. With a sigh, he leaned back in his seat.

"Everything okay?" Darcy idled into the room, then dropped down onto the cushion beside him. He stretched his arms above his head. "All shopped out."

Adrian chuckled.

"So, Abby, what did she want?"

"It was about my Dad's birthday thing."

"Birthday thing? Sounds exciting." He laughed, then squeezed Adrian's knee. "So another Fitzgerald family shindig?"

"Not as grand a size as the wedding, but yes. It's his sixtieth." Adrian raised his head and was surprised to find Darcy looking at him with a smile on his face. "What?"

"Nothing. Just looking." He turned in his seat and rested his elbow on the back of the couch to rest his head in his hand. "So what's the problem? You have *that* look on your face."

"Look?" Adrian flinched a little as Darcy reached forward and tapped him on the end of the nose.

"When your nose crinkles and your lips get pouty."

Adrian folded his arms. He didn't doubt he pulled a face where his family was concerned. "Mom wants Abby to bring her boyfriend to the party."

"Okay, Michael. And?" Darcy frowned, and then it must have hit him that something was badly wrong, and he narrowed his eyes.

"She also might be expecting me to bring someone." He held Darcy's gaze.

Darcy hesitated a moment. "I guess now is not a good time to joke that I can call Bryant & Waites to book Rowan if you like. Probably get you a discount."

Adrian shook his head. "Very funny. You're a funny guy. Not."

"My bad." Darcy cocked his head and ran his tongue around his teeth. "I'm going to guess Abby never told your parents about our contract, did she?"

"No. She's been too busy with work." He air-quoted the too busy, even though it was probably true that she'd been too busy. She was permanently busy.

"And you're worried about dropping that bomb on them at this party?"

"I think Dad would be okay if we handled it right, played it off as a huge joke, but my Mom..." She had born the gossip and dirty looks when he had come out as gay. He didn't want to cause them any further embarrassment in front of other people.

Darcy rested his hand on Adrian's. "Then let's not drop it."

"What? No. I didn't mean…"

He had never been one to hide his relationships. His parents had never expected him to. Despite what anyone else in the family thought, they wanted him to be true to who he was and who he loved. Even if he had terrible taste in men sometimes. *I thought maybe we could have the boyfriend chat, and now he wants me to hide it?*

Darcy squeezed Adrian's hand. "We should invite them over for dinner."

"Seriously?"

"Instead of dropping a bomb, it'll be like pulling the pin on a hand grenade."

Dinner with my parents. Adrian stared at Darcy's hand around his.

"You, your parents, and your *boyfriend* sitting around a table, making small talk, eating food. It'll be fun." Darcy gave Adrian's hand a shake to encourage him.

"My boyfriend."

Darcy placed a hand under his chin and lifted Adrian's head a little so their eyes met. "You're my boyfriend. We're boyfriends. Okay with that?"

"Completely." He was so happy with that.

"Okay, so we settled that, and now we organize a dinner, and we can fill them in on what the situation is and then let them decide if they want me at the party or not."

"Or me," Adrian said. "Are you sure about a dinner here?"

With a shrug, Darcy assured him, "It's fine. I want to clear the air, don't want to cause anyone any problems."

Adrian shook his head. "I meant about the 'me and my boyfriend' part."

There was warmth in Darcy's eyes as he leaned forward. "It's been a few weeks now, so I thought maybe we could make this official. *Us* official." He lifted Adrian's hand to his mouth and pressed a kiss to the back of it. "What do you think?"

Adrian couldn't stop himself from smiling. He sat forward, tugging Darcy by his shirt into a kiss. "I think I should call my Mom and invite her and Dad for dinner."

Chapter Thirteen

DINNER HAD SEEMED LIKE A REALLY GOOD IDEA AT THE TIME.

That was before Adrian went quiet.

Everything had been going according to plan. The apartment was immaculate, the menu arranged, and there were fresh flowers in two vases, one by the door, the other in the front room. Apparently, Adrian's mom had a thing for fresh flowers and how it showed care for a person's environment. All Darcy saw was that the poor things probably only had a week to live at best, but he didn't argue. This might've been his apartment, but tonight was all Adrian's doing.

All that happened was that Abby had texted to say that the dessert she'd been in charge of had been involved in an accident. She didn't elaborate, but from that point on, Adrian had been subdued. He'd gone from walking about the place moving things, then putting them back to sitting on the edge of the sofa with a blank expression. Darcy considered what to do based on the fact this had happened before. Only once, but it was five days ago when he'd called his parents to set up this spill-the-secrets dinner party. When he'd gotten off the phone, he'd gone into the bedroom and sat on the bed. Darcy checked in on him a couple of times, trying to pull him out of the funk, but it hadn't worked.

It was exactly forty-nine minutes until they were due to arrive, and Adrian needed to snap out of things before that. He sat on the small table in front of the sofa, resting his hands on his knees and sighing heavily. That didn't make Adrian look at him, so he did it again, this time with an added *fuck.*

Adrian glanced up at him, blinking in surprise.

"Huh?" he asked.

"I'm worried about tonight," Darcy lied. In reality, he wasn't worried at all. He'd seen some crappy things in his life, and facing parents was low on the list of anxiety-inducing situations. If the worst happened, then Darcy would demand they left his place and never come back. Hopefully it wouldn't come to that; he expected they would understand the farce, the weird coincidences, and would laugh it all off. Darcy would work his hardest to make sure that happened. But yeah, he didn't have anxiety gnawing at him quite the same as Adrian did.

"You are?" Adrian was clearly surprised, and he frowned at Darcy. "I'm sorry. Should we cancel?"

Ah, that wasn't what Darcy was going for at all. He'd been hoping to pull Adrian out of his own head, not create more problems.

"No. We can do this. Nothing will go wrong, but we probably need to get some kissing in before they arrive."

"Kissing?" He quirked a smile as if he'd seen through Darcy's plan. Then they were kissing, and the looming specter of parents plus a dessert that wasn't making it here alive vanished.

. . .

OF COURSE they had to separate when the doorbell sounded, but Darcy had done his bit, and he liked the fact that Adrian's lips were slightly swollen from kissing, and his hair not quite so perfectly flat. That didn't last long because Adrian caught sight of himself in the mirror.

"Oh my god," he gasped quietly, "what did you do?" He patted his hair and held a finger to his mouth.

Darcy pressed one last kiss to Adrian's shoulder; that had to be a safe place, right? Then he helped to straighten Adrian's tie and checked his own one last time. This wasn't like any kind of family dinner he'd ever been to. His experience of family dinners was more turn-up-and-do-what-you-want kind of things. This was all fresh flowers, good crockery, and ties. Bracing himself, he stood back a little and let Adrian open the door.

Abby and Michael entered, and she seemed as stressed as Adrian had been, handing over a covered plate.

"We stopped at the bakery," she announced and watched nervously as Adrian stole a peek.

"Perfect," he said and took whatever it was into the kitchen.

"Darcy," she said and grabbed Michael, pulling him forward, "this is *my* Michael."

Michael had a genuine smile, wore glasses, and grinned broadly. "Nice to meet you at last," he said and pumped Darcy's hand enthusiastically. "Abby has told me so much about you."

They didn't have time for more, Adrian ushering them away from the door and into the living room.

"This is going to go down like a lead balloon," Abby muttered, but Darcy didn't miss that Michael took her hand and gripped it, tugging her close to him. That single action was endearing and perfectly timed.

"We have our stories straight."

"I still don't like this."

The buzzer sounded.

"This is it," Abby murmured.

"Showtime," Adrian added.

They went to the door, and there were air kisses and big hugs from Paula, and she was the one who entered the living room first, with Harvey a few steps behind, after stopping to talk to his children.

She went straight to Darcy, embraced him hard, and they exchanged quick hellos.

"I'm surprised to see you here," she murmured, and Adrian winced. "Are you and Abby back to being a *thing*?"

Then she turned to Michael and opened her arms.

"I'm Paula, and this is Harvey."

"Michael," he said and accepted the hug.

"So nice to meet you, Michael," she said and stood to one side to allow Harvey to shake hands.

"Before dinner, there is something that we need to talk about," Adrian began, and Darcy spotted the gratitude Abby threw his way. Please sit."

"Yes, please, Adrian, I'd like a glass of wine."

"Mom, we wanted to talk first—"

"It's been a long week," Paula said and elbowed Harvey. "We both need a drink."

Darcy held out a hand to stop Adrian. "I've got this."

Drinks in hand, the parents sat, Adrian and Abby sat, and he and Michael did this whole hovering-in-the-background thing. Maybe if he just scooped up Adrian and kissed him soundly again, then they wouldn't have to explain anything at all. He didn't, but he did exchange wary looks with Michael. Adrian had this whole speech in his head, a mess of decisions and realizations that was probably better off being shown as a flow chart. As much as Darcy had encouraged him to just speak naturally, he'd worked out every possible permutation and had it all mapped out in his head.

"Mom, Dad. Darcy is my boyfriend," Adrian blurted.

That was *not* how the news was supposed to be broken. Adrian and Abby had created all kinds of what-if scenarios and decided that gently easing their parents into the deception was to be done carefully. Darcy immediately sat on the arm of the sofa next to Adrian, holding his hand, Michael following suit and drawing Abby close.

"Sorry?" Paula said.

"It's a long story," Adrian began.

This was better. This was getting back on track the way they were supposed to explain things. Still, they'd jumped the gun, given that he was now holding Adrian's hand.

Paula cleared her throat. "Abby, did you know your former boyfriend was…" She waved a hand, and Darcy stiffened. Here came all the questions.

"What, Paula?" he prompted in a calm tone.

"…in love with your brother," she finished and looked as if she was going to cry. "Sweetheart, you were so in love with him, and when you broke up, I felt so sorry for you."

Hang on. What?

Darcy held his tongue, waited for Abby to explain about the rent-a-boyfriend thing, but Abby seemed to be as tongue-tied as Adrian. She stared at Paula as if the woman had sprouted two heads, evidently in shock at the compassion from her mom. So Darcy decided to take matters into his own hands before this got even messier. He was in love with Adrian, Michael and Abby were together, and he just wanted it done.

"Okay, Paula, Harvey, this is what happened. Abby is my friend. She asked me to pretend to be her date to help ease what would have been an excruciatingly bad week for her. We were friends, that is all, and I apologize for the lie, but we did it for her. Through this, I met Adrian, and in the space of the week, I was falling for him, and now we've spent a lot of time together, and I love him, and we're a couple. Also, Abby has always loved Michael, but it took that week for her to see who she really needed to be with."

He stopped then. That summed up the glossed-over version of events that Abby and Adrian had agreed on.

Paula's mouth fell open.

"Harvey?" she managed to say to her husband, pleading for his support.

Harvey pressed a hand to Paula's knee. "Okay, then. Abby is with Michael, Adrian is with Darcy. Excellent. Now is it time for dinner? Whatever you're cooking smells wonderful."

Adrian was the first to move, up and out to the small kitchen, and Abby wasn't far behind, which left him and Michael and the parents, which hardly seemed fair. Paula remained quiet, her mouth still open, but then Michael cleared his throat.

"Mrs. Fitzgerald, Mr. Fitzgerald, I love your daughter. I've loved her for six years, ever since that first day I was assigned to work in the lab with her," he announced. "I want to ask her to marry me, and I would love your blessing." Paula's mouth fell open even farther. "I have my grandmother's ring." He fumbled in his pocket and pulled out a small box, opening it to show Paula, and then the unexpected happened.

Paula cried.

Not loudly. Darcy imagined she was far too refined to sob noisily, but there were bright tears in her eyes, and her hands were twisted in a knot on her lap.

"And you, Darcy?" she asked, her voice thick with emotion.

Was she asking if Darcy was going to propose? Not here and now, no, but yes, one day, when he and Adrian learned each other better. He'd thought maybe Christmas, which was only a few months away. He wasn't going to say that now.

"I love your son," he said. "It's early days, but I can't imagine life without him."

The tears that shone in her eyes coalesced, and a single one of them trickled down her powdered cheek. Then she took her husband's hand and leaned on him.

"My babies are happy," she murmured.

Harvey patted her hand in reassurance. "Seems that way, Paula, seems that way. I do have some questions for young Michael here. Maybe he and I could take a walk to…" They were on the second floor, but then he spotted the patio doors leading to a small balcony. "Out there," he said. Michael went pale but followed his prospective father-in-law closely. When the door shut behind them, Darcy could only imagine the kind of questions Michael was being asked, and he was glad he wasn't out with them.

Only then, he wasn't, because that meant he was alone with Paula. He smiled tentatively, and she narrowed her wet eyes at him.

"You're a very good actor," she announced.

He should be proud of that, right? Because that was his job at the end of the day. He wanted to say thank you but imagined this wasn't where the line of conversation was ending.

"And you can honestly tell me you fell for Adrian in the space of a week?"

"I did. He's a very special man."

"I know he is," she began. Then she stopped and closed her eyes briefly. "I think I'm in shock," she murmured.

"For what it's worth, Abby and Adrian wanted to tell you earlier."

She smiled then and shook her head. "No, they didn't." She stared at him pointedly, daring him to disagree, but there was a hint of a smile on her carefully rouged lips.

"You're right. They didn't."

The smile grew, and Darcy saw the same beauty in her that he saw in both of her children. Tonight was probably going to be awkward and a hundred kinds of weird, but the first hurdle had been cleared.

Michael went to one knee after dessert, "Abby, forget hydrogen. You're my number one element. Not that you can forget hydrogen, but in the context of this proposal—"

"Yes," Abby interrupted.

As proposals went, and Darcy had seen a few in his time, this was perfect for Abby and Michael.

Thankfully, the rest of the evening was focused on weddings and not on deception. When everyone had gone home, when it was just him and Adrian, cuddled up in the big bed, boneless after making love, all Darcy could think was a Christmas proposal was definitely on his own to-do list.

Epilogue

So this is a Fitzgerald Company Christmas party.

Darcy smiled as a silver tray was thrust in his direction. "Thank you," he said and took one of the offered hors d'oeuvre. He twisted the smoked salmon appetizer, appreciating the neat, delicate presentation. It seemed a shame to eat it.

"Whatever." He popped it into his mouth, surprised by the slight kick of chili.

"Having fun?" The voice in his ear was low, sultry, and female.

Darcy turned his head, relaxing a little when he realized who it was. "Abby," he said.

She laughed and patted him on the shoulder. "Scare you?"

"Maybe a little."

Abby nursed a champagne flute to her chest and the light reflected off the diamond in her engagement ring. "So you've been abandoned, I take it?"

"Somebody wanted to talk finances or something equally formal." Darcy shrugged. He didn't remember who, just one of the many nameless relatives or employees of the Fitzgerald family.

"Poor Ade." She sipped her drink.

"No Michael today?"

Abby shook her head. "He made up some story about this annual dinner thing he does with college friends around Christmas."

"College friends, huh?"

"He clearly needs educating on the importance of a Fitzgerald soirée." She edged close enough to bump her shoulder to his. "Though I don't recall seeing you at the more recent gatherings."

Laughing, Darcy cast his gaze around the room. "Work."

"What is it with these completely reasonable excuses?" She sighed as she stared across the room.

"Abby, Darcy, hello."

They both turned to see Charlotte standing there, looking at them. He hadn't seen her since the wedding, although he'd had dinner once with Graham, who'd joyfully announced that Charlotte was pregnant.

The way she stood with her hand on her rounded belly, in a softly tailored, flowing silk dress, her hair loose around her shoulders, she seemed so normal. Her makeup was light, and there was no distress or pain in her eyes.

"I wonder if I could talk to you, Abby," she said. "And you, Darcy, considering you were front and center. Abby, I owe you an apology," she said.

"Charlie—"

"No, please let me talk. I was a bitch. We were trying so hard for a baby, and nothing was working, and he was always at the office, and so busy, and talking to you, and I let my insecurities get the better of me. Can you forgive me?"

She seemed absolutely genuine, and her eyes were bright with emotion.

Abby, on the other hand, evidently didn't know what to do or say, and Darcy decided to step in.

"There's nothing to forgive. We're all happy now," he added. "Right, Abby?"

Abby seemed to read the situation and extended her hands, pulling Charlotte into a hug. "Nothing to forgive. Family stuff is all."

Charlotte hugged Darcy as well. Then with a smile she left them, and for a moment, Darcy felt at peace, knowing that Abby and Charlotte were okay.

"Oh, crap." Abby grabbed Darcy by the arm and dragged him to stand in front of her. "Don't move."

"What?" He glanced over his shoulder. *What now?*

"Don't look." Abby clutched his wrist.

"Who can't I look at?"

"Aunt Vi. Ever since she found out Michael and I were engaged; the condition of my uterus has been the sole topic of conversation."

Darcy raised an eyebrow. "Lovely."

"Ugh." She leaned to one side, aligning her body with Darcy's. "Anyway, speaking of engaged, have you... You know?"

He rested his hand over the pocket of his jacket. He'd been carrying the ring around with him for the last week, trying to decide on the best timing for the proposal. Though anxious as hell, he had done the gentlemanly thing and spoken to Adrian's parents. Harvey Fitzgerald had given his approval with a rare stern expression and an overly firm handshake, and Darcy was under no illusion that, should he dream of hurting Adrian, Harvey would not forgive Darcy.

Paula, on the other hand, had been all teary-eyed and grateful to him for loving Adrian and being good to him.

"Did you get the one you showed me?" Abby's gaze fell to his pocket. "Are you going to do it here?" Her eyes lit up.

Darcy pursed his lips. Adrian wasn't a fan of these large parties, surrounded by people who were as good as strangers. *Maybe when it's only his parents and Abby. Maybe it should be just the two of us.*

"I don't know," he admitted. "I mean, there are a lot of people here."

Abby scanned the room, then downed the last of her drink. "The center of attention. He'd hate it."

"Who'd hate what?"

Abby spluttered when Adrian spoke. Neither she nor Darcy had noticed he had returned. "When did you get back?" She patted her chest.

"Just now." Adrian tilted his head from side to side. "Roger wanted to talk figures for the Lovell contract. Would have dragged me downstairs to the offices if his wife hadn't aided in my escape." He smirked when he realized both Abby and Darcy were wearing the same clueless expression. "Don't ask. Anyway, you were saying about someone hating something. Who were you talking about?"

Darcy opened his mouth, and for the first time in a long time, his mind went blank. He was used to being on the spot through his work, good at improvising his lines and yet…

"Michael," Abby blurted out.

"Michael?"

"Yes, he…he…" She held her glass out in front of her as she struggled to follow through with her tale.

Adrian raised one of his eyebrows expectantly.

Panic rose as a deep shade of pink on Abby's face. She stared past Adrian. "Justin's shirt. If I got him one like that, I don't think he'd wear it. Too pattern-y. He's more a solid pale-blue kind of guy."

Adrian checked behind him, focusing on Justin. "Well, I suppose."

I don't think he's buying this story.

"But yeah. I should probably go...over... Oh, is that Mom? Later, guys." And with that, Abby squeezed through the gap between Darcy and Adrian and scuttled in Paula's direction.

Adrian watched his sister cross the room, then turned to face Darcy. He smiled. "Abby has willingly gone to find Mom? So, are you going to tell me what you were *really* talking about?"

"I don't know what you mean." Darcy pushed his hands into his jacket pockets.

"Justin's shirt. Seriously?"

"I have to agree with Abby. I don't think it'd be Michael's thing really."

Adrian rested his hand on his hip. "Uh huh."

Darcy felt out the contents of the small drawstring pouch in his pocket. He briefly pinched the ring. "Is there anywhere we can go and be just us for a minute?"

"Just us?"

"To talk."

"To talk? As in *talk*?" Adrian's jaw tensed. "Am I about to get dumped? Is this so you don't have to buy me a Christmas present?"

"Wow." Darcy laughed. "And no." He edged forward and rested his hand on Adrian's waist. "I thought you might like some space away from all this." He indicated the other guests in the room.

Adrian pressed his hand to Darcy's chest. "Okay, we can go talk." He trailed his fingers down, catching each of the buttons of Darcy's shirt, then took Darcy by the hand.

Darcy let Adrian lead him through the crowd. He glanced to the side, meeting Abby's eyes. She tilted her head as if to ask a question. Darcy nodded. *Now.* He was going to ask him now.

It seemed Abby understood his intentions. She pressed her palms together and raised her hands to her lips. A wide smile spread across her face as she mouthed something Darcy interpreted as *good luck.*

"Will this do?" Adrian stopped in a small area away from the main function room, seemingly a waiting area consisting of two couches and a water cooler.

Darcy didn't get to reply before he found himself in a kiss.

With a groan, Adrian leaned back. "I needed that."

"Feel better now?"

"You have no idea." Adrian rotated his shoulders and closed his eyes. "It was so noisy in there." He opened his eyes, then stepped back and dropped down on one of the sofas. "We need to suffer through a couple more speeches, and then we should be able to get out of here."

"Freedom," Darcy stated and sat beside Adrian. He fidgeted with the ring, freeing it from the protective pouch. He blinked as Adrian patted his knee.

"You wanted to talk?" Adrian looked at him with an earnest expression.

Darcy nodded. It was as if there was something caught in his throat. *Fuck. How is this so difficult?*

"Is it about something good?" Adrian pressed when Darcy failed to speak.

Again, Darcy nodded.

"Oh, is it about the vacation?" The tension Adrian had

held in his shoulders eased. "Did you work out the dates out with Gideon?"

"Vacation, yes," Darcy said. He had forgotten he needed to tell Adrian everything was arranged for their first real vacation together. Originally, the dates Adrian had to work with clashed with a potential assignment from Bryant & Waites. As it was a new *boyfriend*, Jared, had recently come on the books. He was keen and cheerful, and the job that needed covering seemingly straightforward, so everyone involved was agreeable with them switching.

"That's great." Adrian made an excited squeak as he planted a firm kiss on Darcy's mouth. He deepened the kiss, parting Darcy's lips with his tongue.

Darcy closed his eyes, gently brushed the back of his hand over Adrian's jaw. "I love you," he whispered when Adrian released him from the kiss and pulled him into a tight embrace. With a sigh, he rested his chin on Adrian's shoulder. Leaving the ring in his pocket, he returned the hug, curling his fingers against the back of Adrian's jacket.

Maybe next time.

"Congratulations."

Darcy opened his eyes as he heard the excitement in Abby's voice.

Oh crap. His back was to Abby so there was no way to silence her. He tried to free himself, but Adrian wasn't letting him go so easily.

"Can I see it?"

"See what?" Adrian asked.

"The ring, silly." Abby laughed.

Darcy tried to pull away but was unable to. It was as if Adrian's grip was tightening. As Abby's laugh faded, Darcy tried to imagine the look on both their faces. Adrian's confusion and Abby's regret.

"Wait. He didn't... So you aren't..." The tone of Abby's voice shifted higher. "Then what's with the kissing and the hugging and the stupid smile on your faces?"

"We're going on vacation, and wait a minute. You were spying on us?" Adrian loosened his hold.

"Not spying as such, just... Darcy?"

Darcy sat back. He relaxed his shoulders before raising his head and meeting Adrian's gaze.

"Darcy?" Adrian said.

There was no point in spinning another tale. The truth seemed as good an answer as anything else. "She thought I'd proposed to you. I *was* going to propose to you." He pulled the ring out of his pocket and held it in the palm of his hand. He glanced over his shoulder. "It was harder than I thought, okay?"

"What? Mister Smooth forgot his lines?" Abby pointed her clutch bag in his direction. "This is not the time to have trouble with your performance." She pressed her lips together in a pout. "I need a drink."

Darcy thought to call her back, to get her to help him out of the mess he suddenly found himself in. He sighed and looked back at Adrian who was eyeing the ring.

"Sorry. This wasn't exactly how I'd planned—"

"Ask me," Adrian interrupted.

"What?"

"Ask me." The expression on Adrian's face was like nothing Darcy had ever seen before.

Darcy held the ring between his index finger and thumb. He had lost his chance for romance and surprise. "Adrian Fitzgerald." He took hold of Adrian's hand.

Adrian's eyes shone brightly.

"Will you marry me?"

Adrian remained silent. He smiled as he stared at Darcy's hand around his.

"You're seriously going to do this to me?" Darcy gave a nervous chuckle.

Adrian cupped Darcy's cheek, drawing him into a kiss. "Yes," he whispered against Darcy's lips. "Yes, I'll marry you." He laughed when Darcy pulled him into a hug.

"I love you," Darcy said. He held Adrian tightly.

"Squashing me," Adrian uttered.

Darcy relaxed his hold, allowing room for Adrian to lean back. "Sorry."

Gently, Adrian held Darcy's face. "I'm so glad I got to meet you."

If Abby hadn't come to the office looking for a *boyfriend*. If Darcy hadn't taken the assignment. "Maybe it was written in the stars."

Adrian pressed his palms more firmly to Darcy's face, squeezing his cheeks and causing his lips to pout.

"Erm, Ade?"

Grinning, Adrian guided Darcy close, then kissed him again. They spent a long moment with their lips locked together.

The pressure of Adrian's hands gradually lessened, and Darcy took hold of his wrist. "Here." Darcy slid the ring down Adrian's finger. Relief washed over him as he pushed it down over Adrian's knuckle. The ring fit, just as Adrian had fit so easily into his life.

Adrian turned his hand, threading his fingers between Darcy's. "I love you, too."

GET **the next book in the series - Get Kaden Here**

Next in the Boyfriend For Hire series

Kaden (Boyfriend for Hire 2)

Kaden

When the lines between pretense and reality blur, can the actor and the boyfriend-for-hire discover something real?

Ryan Levesque is Hollywood's newest blue eyed boy. Moving from soap operas to the big screen has paid off for the kid from Minnesota, and he's hot property. But, when a video from the lowest point of his past is shared on social media everything begins to unravel and old hurts resurface. His agent suggests a way out of the mess, and he jumps at the chance to make things right by pretending he's in a committed, loving relationship with the tall, dark, sexy boyfriend for hire, Kaden. Only, he never counted on the impact Kaden would have on his life, or his career.

When Kaden Moore's next assignment lands in his lap, he's expecting nothing more than a self-centered celebrity who's messed up. Kaden's new role is that of Hollywood A-lister Ryan Levesque's boyfriend, a PR stunt concocted by his agents to restore the actor's dented popularity. Kaden is aware of the video that surfaced from Ryan's past, and though it raises questions about what kind of man Ryan is, it's not any of Kaden's business. Kaden has been pretending his entire life, and knows he can show the troublesome actor a thing or two about the world beyond the Hollywood bubble. But maybe Kaden isn't as clued up as he thinks, especially when it comes to the heart and love.

Buy Kaden Here

Sapphire Cay

Sapphire Cay

1. Follow the Sun
2. Under the Sun
3. Chase The Sun
4. Christmas In The Sun
5. Capture The Sun
6. Forever In The Sun

Also from RJ & Meredith

Standalone Christmas

- The Road to Frosty Hollow

Free Reads

- Stronger Together

Meet RJ Scott

RJ discovered romance in books at a very young age and realized that if there wasn't romance on the page, she could create it in her head. With over one hundred and fifty books published, she is a full time author of gay romance.

She lives and works out of her home in the beautiful English countryside, spends her spare time reading, watching films, and enjoying time with her family.

The last time she had a week's break from writing she didn't like it one little bit and has yet to meet a box of chocolates she couldn't defeat.

www.rjscott.co.uk | rj@rjscott.co.uk

NEWSLETTER - rjscott.co.uk/rjnews

facebook.com/author.rjscott

instagram.com/rjscott_author

amazon.com/author/rj-scott

bookbub.com/authors/rj-scott

goodreads.com/rjscott

patreon.com/RJScott

Meet Meredith Russell

Meredith Russell lives in the heart of England. An avid fan of many story genres, she enjoys nothing less than a happy ending. She believes in heroes and romance and strives to reflect this in her writing. Sharing her imagination and passion for stories and characters is a dream Meredith is excited to turn into reality.

www.meredithrussell.co.uk
meredithrussell666@gmail.com

facebook.com/meredithrussellauthor

x.com/MeredithRAuthor

instagram.com/miss_meredith_r